Chestnut Hill
Chasing Dreams

700034239654

Also by Lauren Brooke:

Chestnut Hill
The New Class
Making Strides
Heart of Gold
Playing for Keeps
Team Spirit
All or Nothing

The *Heartland* Series

Chestnut Hill
Chasing Dreams

Lauren Brooke

■SCHOLASTIC

With special thanks to
Elisabeth Faith

Scholastic Children's Books
An imprint of Scholastic Ltd
Euston House, 24 Eversholt Street, London, NW1 1DB, UK
Registered office: Westfield Road, Southam, Warwickshire, CV47 0RA
SCHOLASTIC and associated logos are trademarks and or registered
trademarks of Scholastic Inc.

First published in the UK by Scholastic Ltd, 2008

Copyright © Working Partners, 2008

10 digit ISBN 1 407 10484 5
13 digit ISBN 978 1407 10484 3

British Library Cataloguing-in-Publication Data
A CIP catalogue record for this book is available from the British Library

The right of Lauren Brooke to be identified as the author of this work
has been asserted by her.

All rights reserved
This book is sold subject to the condition that it shall not, by way of
trade or otherwise, be lent, hired out or otherwise circulated in any form
of binding or cover other than that in which it is published. No part of
this publication may be reproduced, stored in a retrieval system, or
transmitted in any form or by any means (electronic, mechanical,
photocopying, recording or otherwise) without the prior written
permission of Scholastic Limited.

Printed by CPI Bookmarque, Croydon, CR0 4TD
Papers used by Scholastic Children's Books are made from wood
grown in sustainable forests.

1 3 5 7 9 10 8 6 4 2

This is a work of fiction. Names, characters, places, incidents and dialogues
are products of the author's imagination or are used fictitiously. Any
resemblance to actual people, living or dead, events or locales is entirely
coincidental.

www.scholastic.co.uk/zone

Chapter One

"We're here!" Mr Harper announced. He steered the car through the ornate iron gates, which had a chestnut tree with spreading roots and branches worked into them, along with the profile of a horse's head.

Honey Harper couldn't believe that an entire year had passed and she was returning to Chestnut Hill as an eighth-grader. She didn't know who she was most looking forward to seeing after a whole summer's vacation. She'd missed her friends like crazy: Dylan, Malory, Lani. But it had been just as tough being apart from her favourite four-legged friend in the entire world. *Moonlight Minuet*. Honey closed her eyes and pictured the beautiful dappled-grey mare.

"Hey, you're not going to sleep on us, are you?" Honey's twin brother nudged her and called out to their parents. "Mum, Dad, maybe you should think about swapping Honey's school. It's sent her to sleep already!"

"Joker." Honey opened her eyes and yanked down Sam's baseball cap so the peak covered his face. She leaned out of the open window to get a better view. *My school*, she thought with a shiver that was half excitement and half pride. Last year she hadn't known what to expect as she'd headed up the tree-lined drive for the first time. She'd wondered if she'd make friends, or if she'd be so homesick that she'd want to leave before the end of the first term. This time she couldn't wait to get to Adams House and see her new room and catch up with all her friends.

Old House came into view, standing amid immaculate green lawns at the top of the hill that gave the school its name. Honey smiled. Back home in England, architecture had to date back to Tudor times before it qualified as old. Although she had to admit that the white colonial building which housed the faculty and administration offices looked pretty stunning against the backdrop of autumn colours.

Honey sat back in her seat so she could slip her shoes on. She wanted to be ready to jump out the moment her dad stopped the car.

"It's a shame there's not a rope for you to swing out of the window. It would cut back on the time needed to open the door." Sam, as ever, was right on her wavelength.

"True. I don't think much of the extras the car salesman threw in when Dad bought the car," Honey agreed.

"An ejector button would be even better." Sam pretended to be serious. "That way you wouldn't even have to worry about fighting your way through hundreds of bodies to reach your dorm. You could just sail right in through the window."

"Hey." Honey wagged her finger. "Fighting my way

through hundreds of bodies is tradition. It's like a rite of passage."

"What happens if you don't do it? Are you forbidden entry to the dorm midnight feasts?" Sam teased.

"I'm sure none of those go on at Chestnut Hill." Mrs Harper turned around to smile at them. "Mrs Herson strikes me as someone who makes sure the school rules are carried out to the letter."

Honey thought of her housemother, who was firm, but whose eyes frequently twinkled with humour. It was true that she hadn't taken kindly to their midnight feast and game of truth or dare during the first term. *But then, things did get way out of hand when Dylan took up Lynsey's dare to do a midnight jumping session on Morello.*

Honey was distracted from thoughts of the previous year as her dad pulled in behind a long line of cars and MPVs. She jumped out of the car and scanned the crowded steps in front of Adams House.

"Honey!" Through the throng of girls and parents someone was shrieking her name.

Honey shaded her eyes from the afternoon sun. Between the crowds she caught a glimpse of waving hands and a flash of bright-red hair. "Dylan!" Honey squeezed her way towards her friend. "It's so good to see you!" she exclaimed. "Look at how tanned you are!"

"I'm not the only one who's caught the sun," Dylan said, standing back to admire Honey's pale-gold skin. "I thought England did sleet, not heat?"

"Four entire weeks without rain," Honey declared triumphantly.

"What's this? A reunion without us?" demanded a voice in Honey's ear. She would recognize that Midwest drawl anywhere.

"Lani!" she cried, spinning around to give her friend a hug. Lani was wearing a fringed suede jacket and a baseball cap, and her naturally tanned skin was the colour of a beechnut. Malory stood beside her, with a backpack slung over her shoulder and a bag of riding boots at her feet.

"We've been waiting for you," Malory explained. "We didn't want to say hi to the horses until you arrived."

"Although you have no idea how close the horses came to winning out," Lani said with her usual dry humour. She glanced over Honey's shoulder. "Hey, it's good to see your brother acknowledging his place as your private valet."

Honey turned to see Sam staggering towards them, loaded up with cases. "Don't be sucked in by how many he's carrying. He's picked the lightest ones!"

Her friends had met Sam the previous term under very different circumstances. In fact, Lani's first meeting with Honey's twin had been at the local hospital, where he had been receiving treatment for leukaemia. *Thank goodness, he's so much better now.*

"I like to think of it as being gallant, but after that comment, maybe sucker would be a better description," he retorted, dropping two of the cases at Honey's feet.

"Much as I love your attempt to assimilate American lingo, I think you'll find 'sucker' got gunned down by the

4

style police aeons ago," Lani teased. "There are lots of other, much better, names we could give you."

"Time out, you two!" Malory laughed and made a T-shape with her hands.

"Talking of which, you still haven't taken me to a baseball game, Lani." Sam flexed his arms and groaned. "My knuckles are going to be dragging along the ground after I've finished carrying all this stuff."

Lani picked up one of the cases. "This feels as light as a feather to me. You're out of condition, my friend. It must have been all those days lazing about eating cream teas." She delivered the last line in her best take of an English accent.

"Terrible." Sam shook his head sadly. "Look, why don't we swap email addresses? That way you can give me a time and date when you finally make good on your promise to take me to a game, and I can arrange to give you some lessons on delivering a proper English accent."

"Only if you learn the list of modern lingo I'll send to you. I'm not risking going to a game with someone who might shout out 'sucker' at one of the players." Lani grinned.

Honey's parents caught up with them. Mr Harper was shouldering Honey's carryall, which contained all of her riding kit.

"Sorry, Dad. I got so carried away with seeing everyone again that I forgot about my bags," Honey apologized.

"No problem," her dad said. "Hey, everyone. It's great to see you all again. Did you have a good summer?"

"Fantastic, thanks." Dylan was the first to respond.

"I stayed at home but got to come here and ride Tybalt most days," Malory said, mentioning her favourite horse on the yard. Honey knew that Malory had turned down the chance to train on the prestigious Cavendish riding programme that summer to spend time with her dad. If her wide smile was anything to go by, then she'd made the right decision and had a great vacation.

"We've dumped our bags in the foyer. We figured we'd go down to the horses before finding our new rooms," Dylan told Honey.

"It's a shame they couldn't have found you rooms above the stables," said Sam.

"Above?" Lani blinked. "What would be wrong with us sharing their stalls?"

"Could you imagine me rooming with Morello?" Dylan chuckled. "We'd fight over the best food and he'd end up holding a rooftop protest!"

Honey giggled as she pictured herself being Minnie's roomie. She didn't know what was more amusing, the thought of the beautiful Arab x Connemara mare wearing a pair of pyjamas or Morello sitting up on the barn roof waving a banner. "I'll just dump my bags with yours," she told her friends. "Then we can start measuring up the horses' stalls."

She followed her parents and Sam through the large glass doors that opened into the foyer. It smelled of floor wax and freshly cut flowers. In the centre of the hall Mrs Herson was busy allocating rooms to nervous-looking seventh-graders, although Honey wondered how the housemother was making herself heard over all the commotion.

She helped her dad stack her bags underneath the noticeboard. A poster in bold colours advertised the forthcoming Homecoming Dance, but right now all Honey could think about was having to say goodbye to her family.

"I always hate leaving you, but it helps knowing how happy you are here." Mrs Harper's voice was muffled as she wrapped her arms around Honey and held her close. Honey breathed in her familiar Anaïs Anaïs perfume and closed her eyes. "I'm going to miss you, Mum."

Mrs Harper's eyes were misty when she finally released Honey.

"Have a wonderful time, sweetheart." Mr Harper drew Honey close and dropped a kiss on top of her head. "We'll phone later to make sure you've settled in OK. Would it sound totally corny if I told you that we're missing you already?"

"Totally," Honey replied before giving him another quick hug. Saying goodbye to Sam was next – always the hardest part.

For one moment she caught a look of sadness on her twin's face; Sam didn't have to put what he was feeling into words. Honey knew he'd miss her as much as she would miss him. "Take care of you," he murmured as he gave her a swift hug.

"Take care of you more," she returned.

Mr Harper marshalled her mum and brother out of the foyer.

"Don't have so much fun that you forget to call me," Sam called as he gave a final wave.

Honey watched them go and deliberately steered her thoughts into more positive channels so she wouldn't do anything so seventh grade as burst into tears. *Minnie's waiting for me.* She unzipped the pack of horse cookies she'd stowed in the front pocket of her holdall and then hurried outside, where her friends were waiting for her.

"It felt like you were in Antarctica, not the UK," Dylan told Honey as they walked down the path. "You were sooo out of circulation."

Honey thought of her gran's cosy cottage, which had never housed anything more technical than an iron. She knew that the others had all kept in touch through IM-ing each other, but all she'd been able to do was send her friends a postcard each week. She'd been gutted that she'd accidentally left her mobile phone on her bedside table at home so she couldn't swap text messages.

"Hey!" A girl with jet-black hair in a long plait ran after them. Honey didn't recognize her; she guessed she was a seventh-grader, though she seemed pretty confident as she stood in front of them, blocking their way. "Didn't you hear me calling you?" she demanded.

Honey swapped a glance with Malory, taken aback at the girl's offhand tone.

"The fact that we didn't answer you would sort of suggest that we didn't," Lani said.

"Don't patronize me just because I'm new." The girl crossed her arms and stared at Lani. "I bet you had people help you out when you first came here."

"You're absolutely correct," Dylan beamed. "I would like to apologize on behalf of us all. What would you like us to give you a hand with?"

"All I wanted was to know the way to Adams," the girl sniffed.

The dorm house was only just out of sight, behind a row of trees. Dylan peered into the distance in the opposite direction. "Sure, no problem. Go back to the main drive and fork left. At the chapel, fork right and follow the path around to the right. Stay on the path and you'll end up at Adams House. Have a nice day now."

"Whatever." The girl shrugged before turning on her heel.

Honey could hardly wait for the girl to disappear out of earshot. "I should feel sorry for her but her ego stepped between me and my sympathy!"

"Ditto," Lani said, staring after the girl. "I think you went easy on her by sending her to Potter dorm, Dyl. I'd have sent her all the way over to Saint Kits!"

"It wasn't just the three of us you were out of touch with during the vacation," Lani went on, nudging Honey. "I bet Josh wasn't exactly turning somersaults about you disappearing for the entire summer."

Honey felt herself going red at the mention of her boyfriend's name. "Actually, we did get to meet up mid," she admitted. "He was touring Europe with his grandparents and they stopped off in England for a week to visit some castles."

"No way!" Malory exclaimed.

"You kept that quiet," Dylan remarked.

"I wanted to wait until I saw you," Honey admitted. "It's not something I could fit on to a postcard."

"You're telling me," Lani agreed. "So what did you guys do?"

"Josh stayed in a hotel nearby for two nights." Honey's grandmother had invited Josh and his family around for a barbecue on one of the evenings and some of Sam and Honey's old friends had come over. They had ended the night playing a game of rugby on the village green. When it had grown dark, they'd played on, using the light from the old-fashioned street lamps that fringed the area. Honey smiled. She couldn't wait to see Josh more regularly now he was just a few miles away at Saint Kits. "Hey," she said. "Did I tell you that Sam's going to start at Saint Kits after Christmas?"

"I wondered if he would now he's better." Lani's eyes brightened with interest. "Why isn't he starting straight away?"

"He's been homeschooled over the summer and my mum hopes to get him fully caught up with the rest of the eighth grade by December. He's got private tutors set up, too, so hopefully he'll be up to speed after the Christmas holiday," Honey told them.

Malory reached out and squeezed her arm. "I'm so glad for you, Honey," she said, her blue eyes filled with empathy. Malory's own mother had died a few years ago and Honey knew that her friend could totally understand what she'd gone through with Sam.

"Thanks, Mal." She linked arms with Malory as they

walked off the main path and took a shortcut past the Director of Riding's house. "So you got to do a lot of riding this summer?"

Malory nodded. "Tybalt's coming on so well and we even competed in the Cheney Falls Horse Show! The only time I didn't get to ride was when Dad and I went away camping. It was the first vacation we've had together since Mum. . ." She paused and then put a brighter note into her voice. "It's great that Dad's shop is doing well enough for him to put in a manager when he needs a bit of time off."

Dylan giggled. "I loved the picture you emailed of your dad falling off the decking into the lake."

"How did you and Tybalt do at the show?" Honey asked.

"We won the open jumping," Malory admitted shyly.

"That's fantastic!" Honey exclaimed. It was typical of Malory not to have mentioned her win. "Ms Carmichael must have been psyched!" The Director of Riding had always given Malory and Tybalt total support, even when Tybalt's unpredictable behaviour had made his future at the school uncertain.

"Out of her and my dad, I don't know who was cheering the loudest when we cleared the final double," Malory said with a grin.

Honey knew that Malory could have achieved even more success if she had competed on the A circuit that summer with the Cavendish Programme, but she seemed totally content with the choice she had made to stay home with her dad.

"Did either of you get to do any riding?" she asked Dylan and Lani. "I feel like it's been so long since I got on a horse that I won't know my right rein from my left!"

"We went on a trek through the rainforest when we stayed in Martinique," Dylan told her. "It was amazing. Dad and I went sailing, yachting, scuba diving, canoeing – the whole lot. Can you believe my mom preferred to stay at the hotel and top up her tan?"

They walked along the path that passed the main stable block. All of the doors were open and Honey could smell the disinfectant that had been used to scrub out the stalls.

"It was a father and daughter vacation for us, too," Lani said. "We stayed on a ranch in Alberta and rode out on a cattle drive."

Dylan pretended to look horrified. "Lynsey was right all along!" she gasped. "You *are* a cowgirl!"

"And what's wrong with that?" Lani challenged, putting her hands on her hips.

"There they are!" Malory exclaimed, interrupting their mock argument. They'd reached the path that led to the turnout paddocks, giving a clear view across tidy green fields full of ponies grazing in the autumn sunshine.

Honey ran with her friends down to the first gate. She balanced on the middle bar while searching for Minnie. It didn't take long to spot her. The mare's striking dappled coat and showy looks meant that she stood out easily.

"Minnie!" Honey cupped her hands and called.

Dylan, Malory and Lani had the same idea and the medley of names being shouted made all the horses throw up their heads.

"Min, Min, Min," Honey chanted, waving to the mare. She felt a rush of delight when Minnie whinnied. She hadn't even been sure if Minnie would recognize her. Moonlight Minuet wasn't her horse, after all. She belonged to Patience Duvall, one of Honey's classmates, but was on loan to Ms Carmichael until Patience's riding improved.

I shouldn't have doubted the strength of our bond, Honey realized as Minnie trotted towards her. She had helped to nurse Minnie when the mare had suffered strained tendons; the pony's generous, loving nature meant that she'd never forgotten the hours Honey had spent tending her.

"Hello, angel," Honey said, offering her a horse cookie before slipping her arms around Minnie's neck. She breathed in the horsey smell and tangled her fingers in Minnie's thick mane. *Heaven!*

Minnie nodded her head up and down and then rubbed her temple against Honey's shoulder.

"Do you have an itch?" Honey scratched the short hair above Minnie's eye and smiled as the mare gave a contented sigh. She wished she had a brush so she could sweep it over Minnie's soft coat and work it through her mane and tail so they fell like curtains of silk. She contented herself with teasing out a burr that was tangled in Minnie's forelock. "There," she said and dropped a kiss on Minnie's forehead. "It's out."

Tybalt and Colorado had joined them by the gate and were enjoying a similar amount of attention from Malory and Lani.

"By the time you get here all the cookies will have gone," Dylan called out to Morello, who was still ambling across the field. Honey grinned as the paint-coloured pony broke into a trot like he'd understood what Dylan had said.

"Steady," Malory warned as Colorado, impatient for another cookie, jostled Tybalt. The dark-brown gelding's ears flashed back and he gave Colorado a warning graze with his teeth. Colorado ran back several paces. "Hey, there's no need for that," Malory scolded Tybalt. "Remember your manners, please."

"Colorado, come on back here before you get a rep for being the biggest wimp on campus." Lani held out her hand to the buckskin gelding.

Honey rolled her eyes at Minnie. "Typical boys, always getting into fights!" Minnie nodded as if she agreed.

"Finally!" Dylan congratulated Morello as he joined them at the gate and looked hopefully for a treat. "There you go." She fed him a horse cookie and scratched under his forelock as he crunched his treat.

Suddenly Malory let out a gasp. "Have you seen the time? We'd better head back to the dorm. We haven't even unpacked and convocation's at three!"

"Have you had a chance to see who your roomies are?" Honey asked, giving Minnie one last hug. This year they'd be sharing two to a room.

14

"Not yet," Dylan replied. "I hope the four of us end up being paired off. Surely Mrs Herson knows that would make sense?"

At Adams House the girls had to push their way through the group of ninth-graders looking at the list of room allocations on the bulletin board. Honey scanned the eighth-grade list and felt a flood of relief when she saw her name alongside Lani's. "You and I get to be roomies!" she exclaimed to Lani.

"Yay!" Lani threw her arms around her. "We've totally lucked out!"

Honey hugged her back. *This is such a perfect start!*

"I'm with Alexandra Cooper," Malory announced. "That's great. I'd geared myself up for missing out on her company." She had shared a room with Alexandra and Lani the year before.

Dylan was staring at the list with an expression of horror. "Please, please, pleeeaze tell me I'm seeing things," she said.

Honey checked the list. And gulped. Right alongside Dylan's name, printed in bold type, was the person Dylan would least want to share a room with in the entire school.

Lynsey Harrison!

Chapter Two

"Cheer up, Dyl. It's not every girl that gets free style advice twenty-four-seven." Lani's shot at sympathy was betrayed by her grin.

Malory slipped her arm through Dylan's. "It would have been great to be roomies this year, but we'll still get to spend lots of time together."

"Yeah, and last year we never let room residency bother us." Honey did her best to sound cheerful. "I bet that by the end of the week we'll have room-hopped so much our dorm will be suffering an identity crisis." She knew how difficult it had to be for Dylan to contemplate another year of rooming with Lynsey. *The only thing they can agree on is that they can never agree.*

Lynsey's voice cut through the air. "I don't believe it! I was hoping that this term I'd get to room with somebody who is actually a signed-up member of civilized society."

"Trust me, I didn't put in a request slip for this," Dylan told her. "But I guess if Morello and Bluey can be barn mates, we can cope."

"Bluegrass would never share a stall with that coloured pony. It's bad enough that he has to share the same building." Lynsey gave an exaggerated shiver.

"Let's grab our bags and see what our new rooms are like," Malory put in before Dylan could reply.

"Looking at the chain stores Lynsey's bagged up, space is going to be an issue whatever room we end up in," Dylan said gloomily as she nodded at the heap of bags that Lynsey had set down alongside her cases.

"Dylan, you might do chain stores, but I only do boutiques," Lynsey said as she pulled up the handle of her oversized suitcase. "I did some serious new-season shopping last week. My father insisted, as a reward for all the firsts I brought home on the A circuit. I've got some fabulous stuff and it's all going to have to be hung up. There's no way I'm putting any of it into drawers."

"That's fine by me," Dylan shot back. "I can hitch up a line and hang my stuff along the walls. I'm all for easy access."

Lynsey wrinkled her nose. "You might have lived that way over the summer but there's no way you're turning our room into your wardrobe. It's bad enough I have to be offended by it each time you walk by."

"Hey, speaking of wardrobes, check out Tiger Woods' sidekick." Lani's eyes widened as she stared over at the entrance.

Oh my goodness, what is Patience wearing! Honey stared as Minnie's owner, Patience Duvall, hurried over to greet Lynsey. Patience was wearing close-fitting trousers in blue and white check, a matching sweater over a white collared tee, and a pale blue sun visor. Her shoes looked like streamlined trainers with pointed toes, with a distinctive GTX logo on the side. It only took a moment for Honey to realize what the outfit reminded her of. *She's dressed to play golf!* Patience's dad was walking across the foyer carrying two heavy cases. A blue and silver leather golf bag was slung over his shoulder, each club wearing a neat leather sock.

"Looks like golf is going to be Patience's thing this term," Dylan murmured.

Honey felt a quick leap of hope at the prospect of Patience becoming absorbed in a completely different sport. *Maybe she won't be so interested in working on her riding to get Minnie back.*

Lynsey kissed her friend and Mr Duvall on both cheeks.

"I can see you kicking off a whole new craze. Those shoes would totally rock with skinny jeans." Lynsey's voice carried over as she stood back to admire Patience's outfit. "It's one hundred per cent preppy! You're at boiling point on the fashion thermometer right now."

Patience tweaked her visor so it sat at more of an angle over her shoulder-length light-brown hair. She smiled up at her father. "Dad and I are sooo switched on to golf. We've been having lessons all summer at our club."

"I've developed enough arm strength to tackle Patience's suitcase challenge." Mr Duvall laughed, indicating the cases at his feet.

Honey had always liked Patience's father. She'd first met him when he'd come to the school to oversee the delivery of Minnie. Mr Duvall had made a real effort to talk to them about Patience's new pony, assuming they were all good friends.

"Patience!" Wei Lin ran lightly down the staircase. "You and I are roomies this term!"

Honey noticed disappointment flit over Patience's face. She glanced at Lynsey, who gave a quick shrug. "I'm rooming with Dylan."

"Hi, Mr Duvall." Wei Lin smiled at Patience's father, who just happened to be her all-time favourite author. Honey remembered how psyched she'd been when Mr Duvall had presented her with a set of signed books at a school charity auction. "I've already put out your books on the shelf over my bed. They were the first thing I unpacked."

"That's great," Mr Duvall responded. "I'll make sure to send you my next book that's due out at Christmas, so keep a space for it!"

"Fantastic!" Wei Lin's eyes shone. "Do you want a hand with some of those cases?"

"I'm good, thanks," Mr Duvall told her. "Do you want to lead the way?"

"You could help me with some of my cases," Lynsey chipped in.

"No worries," Wei Lin agreed.

As they walked up the grand curving staircase, Patience's voice carried down. "I'd like to get my golf handicap down to below twenty this year. Dad's arranging for a golf pro to come out to the school to carry on with my training."

Honey smiled at Lani. "I can't wait to see our new room. It's going to be so much fun sharing for the year."

"Totally," Lani agreed. She picked up her one case and shoulder bag. Lani always travelled the lightest of them all.

Honey looked at her own pile of cases and realized that she'd need a few trips to carry them up to her room.

"I'll come back with you to get the rest of them," Lani told her.

"Thanks," Honey said.

They walked up the staircase and Honey felt a shiver of excitement as they walked down the corridor and went through the double doors that opened on to the eighth-grade wing.

"Nine, eight, seven," Lani began counting down the room numbers as they hurried down the corridor. "This is us!" She stopped outside room five.

"I'm opposite you," Malory said. "If we prop open the doors we can pretend we're sharing one big room!"

"I'm the next room down," Dylan told them, nodding her head at the stack of cases and bags left out in the corridor. "Wish me luck!"

"Good luck!" Honey and Lani echoed as they pushed the door to their room open.

"This is so great," Honey enthused. Sunlight poured in through the large windows and danced on the mellow oak furnishings in the room. She dropped her bags on the floor and went to the window to check out the view. Acres of parkland stretched into the distance. The trees were just beginning to spill their leaves to form pools of colour at the base of their trunks. Over to the left were the campus buildings with their network of paths; Honey imagined how lovely it would be seeing them lit up at night.

Honey turned back to the room. She and Lani both had their own drawers, desks and wardrobes and a shared double dressing table. The door to their en-suite bathroom acted as a divider between the two sets of furniture.

"It feels like just yesterday we were unpacking for the first day of term," Lani commented. "But it also seems like aeons ago." She shook her head. "What do you make of the seventh-graders? Did we ever look that lost?"

"Well, thanks to Dylan, some of them are more lost than others," Honey reminded her. "Let's just hope the walk gave her a chance to reassess her attitude!"

"If she doesn't then it's going to make for some interesting moments when we have to share space in the common room," Lani mused as she picked up her bags and walked over to the bed on the left of the room. "Do you mind if I have this one?"

"Help yourself," Honey told her. She unzipped her hand luggage. At the top of the bag was a framed photo wrapped in tissue paper. Honey carefully pulled it out. She smiled at the shot of Minnie taken at sunset in the paddock, and set it down on her bedside table. "Now this place really feels like home!"

"Is it me or should Marshy send out a search party to locate her sense of humour?" Dylan groaned as she unhooked Morello's tack off the wall. "It's only Monday afternoon but I feel like I've put in a week's worth of effort."

Honey had to admit that science had been pretty tough that morning and Mrs Marshall had seemed determined to crack the whip right from their very first lesson. It seemed their teachers wanted to impress the need for eighth grade to be taken seriously. She reached up for Minnie's saddle and bridle, enjoying the feel of the soft supple leather in her hands. "At least we'll get to chill out for the next hour." Riding was a lot higher up her list of favourite subjects than chemistry!

Sarah and Kelly had caught the horses that were being used for the lesson. Each stall had a pony looking expectantly over the door. Minnie was a real people pony and she gave her door an impatient kick when she saw the girls walk out of the tack room.

Honey hurried up the centre aisle of the barn. "Hold your horses, I'm coming!"

"Dylan, Morello's in the feed store!" Tessa Harding yelled. "He and Paris are battling over a sack of pony nuts. Can you come give us a hand?"

Dylan raced towards the feed room. Very occasionally, whoever was putting Morello into his stall would forget to kick over the bottom clasp. The pony was a master at pulling back the top bolt with his teeth and, without the lower clasp secured, he'd be out of his stall the moment he thought he had a clear run at the food store.

"Hello, gorgeous," Honey greeted Minnie. She gently scratched the pony's nose. Minnie nibbled at Honey's sleeve. "I'd love to play with you all afternoon." Honey selected a body brush from her grooming kit. "But we've got a riding lesson to get ready for."

Minnie half closed her eyes as Honey removed the dust stains from her white coat. "Hey, don't fall asleep on me," she teased. But the moment she started tacking up, the mare opened her eyes and lifted her head. Honey straightened Minnie's forelock and stepped back to admire her dished part-Arab face. "Beautiful," she declared.

As Honey led Minnie up the centre aisle she overheard Dylan scolding Morello. "Aunt Ali is going to be mad at us for being late. The next time you decide to pull one of your Houdini stunts, can you make sure it's not before one of my lessons?" Even though Ms Carmichael was Dylan's aunt, the Director of Riding never showed the least bit of favouritism.

"Do you need a hand?" Honey halted Minnie and peered over Morello's door.

Dylan was wrestling with the bridle while Morello tugged at his haynet, oblivious to her stress. "Whoever cleaned his bridle last didn't buckle the straps back in the right holes," Dylan complained. "And his bit was on back to front. There," she did up the cheek strap, "I'm done. Thanks for the offer."

"No worries. See you in the ring."

Honey clicked to Minnie. As they moved away Dylan's voice carried after them. "Morello, spit out the hay! How am I supposed to get the bit in when your mouth's packed tighter than a can of sardines?"

Once they were out on the yard, Honey tightened the girth and swung up into the saddle. Most of the class were already in the arena, warming up at a trot. Lynsey was leading the group on Bluegrass, who had his neck arched and his tail held high. Honey waited for the other riders to go by and then joined in behind Jo-Ann Swelby. The talented rider from Meyer had Skylark working in a beautiful outline.

Honey had to keep her legs on Minnie to encourage the mare to engage her hindquarters. The moment she eased the contact, Minni began to lose impulsion. "Come on, Min," Honey encouraged as she changed the rein. "Wake up, there's a good girl."

They were working on a serpentine when Dylan rode in on Morello.

"You're late," Ms Carmichael called out.

"Sorry. I had a bit of trouble getting ready," Dylan replied. Her cheeks were flushed and Honey saw a wisp of hay sticking out from the side of Morello's mouth, like he was saving a snack for later.

"I'm about to begin the class. You can warm up at the far end." Ms Carmichael didn't give Dylan a chance to go into detail. "Everyone else ride into the centre."

Honey rode Minnie into the middle of the school and reached down to pat the mare when she halted squarely. Malory and Tybalt halted alongside and Honey noticed how patiently the gelding was standing. Last term he would have been shifting his weight and swishing his tail. *He's come such a long way.*

"Welcome back, everyone," Ms Carmichael began

with a warm smile. "I hope you all had a good vacation. I'm sure your batteries are fully charged and you're all set for some real hard work. I'm looking forward to seeing some star performances from our new teams this term. Now, I can either give you the welcome back talk that I drafted earlier or we can skip right through to doing some riding. It's your choice." Ms Carmichael's twinkling blue eyes showed that she knew exactly how much they were all itching to begin the class.

As Honey prepared Minnie to walk forward, Ali Carmichael announced, "It's just flatwork today, so to get you sitting nice and deep, I'd like you to quit your stirrups and cross them over the saddle. Just use half of the school, please. Lynsey, you can lead."

"She's gotta be kidding," Tessa Harding complained in a low voice. "Does she know how little riding I've done this summer? I bet I slide off before Flight completes one loop of the arena." She flipped a section of the pure-grey mare's mane over so it all lay straight.

"If anyone falls off, I'll expect them to attend practice sessions without their stirrups for one hour each night after study hall until they improve," Ms Carmichael said calmly, overhearing.

Honey bit back a grin. She crossed her stirrups and relaxed into Minnie's stride.

"Morello!" Dylan's voice cut through the air. "Will you quit fooling around?"

Honey glanced to the far end of the school to see the paint gelding tucking his nose into his chest and running backwards. Dylan used her legs strongly to get Morello back under control.

"That's enough of a warm up, Dylan. Join in at the rear," Ms Carmichael called.

What is with Morello? Honey wondered.

"Canter when you reach the corner," Ms Carmichael called to Lynsey.

Honey concentrated on giving plenty of space to Malory and Tybalt in front. She didn't want to overcrowd them when it came to her turn to canter. The dark-brown gelding struck off on the correct leg when he reached the corner and tossed his head with enthusiasm at the increase in pace.

"Your turn," Honey whispered as she sat deep and squeezed Minnie. But instead of breaking into a canter, Minnie just trotted faster.

"Try again in the next corner," Ms Carmichael called.

Honey squeezed Minnie even harder and gave the lightest of touches with her whip. To her relief the mare struck off and cantered smoothly down the school.

"Don't forget that most of the horses have been ridden by lots of other riders this summer and most of those were at novice level. You might well have to work hard to get them back into the intermediate groove," Ali Carmichael called out.

No kidding! Honey's legs already felt like jell-o!

By the end of the lesson it wasn't just Honey's legs that were hurting. It felt like every muscle had been stretched and then snapped back into place. It wasn't until Ms Carmichael had them each canter a figure of eight that Minnie really began responding to Honey's signals. Honey wanted to burst into a cheer as she felt the mare come fully on to the bit. Minnie's hind legs worked powerfully, which made her canter full of energy but light at the same time. When they came to a halt Honey bent down to whisper in Minnie's ear, "That was great, well done!"

Paris, Malory, Dylan and Lynsey were still to ride their figure of eight. Paris Mackenzie looked relaxed on her own pony, Whisper. The grey mare completed the figure of eight without any mistakes, and after they had halted, Paris patted the pony's neck.

Lynsey was up next and rode a perfect figure of eight. Bluegrass was calm and collected. His neck was arched and his ears pricked as he gave one hundred per cent to the task at hand. Lynsey sat deep and looked totally poised. *Every bit the A circuit rider.*

Malory and Tybalt began their figure of eight on the wrong leg, but Malory quickly encouraged the gelding to put in a flying change. "Well done," Ms Carmichael called.

Honey admired how quietly Malory sat and allowed Tybalt to get on with the job. *Last term he was so sharp he only seemed to have potential as a showjumper. It's starting to look as if flatwork could be his thing too.*

"Mal's done a fantastic job with Tybalt," Honey whispered to Lani, who had Colorado halted alongside her.

Lani nodded. "She never stopped believing in him," she murmured. She leaned forward to stroke Colorado's neck. "But he's shown us all how right she was."

"Dylan," Ms Carmichael called.

Morello started well, but when they reached the middle of the school, he began to fight Dylan's hands. He carried his head high, and when Dylan rode him more strongly to try to bring the gelding back on the bit, Morello began to shake his head in protest.

Honey's heart went out to Dylan. Morello often had his moments – it was part of his cheeky personality. But it was unusual for him not to have settled down for Dylan. Honey knew how much Dylan had her hopes pinned on winning a full place on the junior jumping team this year instead of her old reserve position.

"You'll have to work hard to bring him up to standard after a summer off intermediate level," was all Ms Carmichael said before she walked across to stand in front of the class. "I'll be sending out this year's schedule in the next couple of days. You'll be having two dressage lessons a week with Mr Musgrave this term, plus a general session with me for your other lesson. Don't forget that in ninth grade you'll get your first chance to transfer to Advanced Riding Classes, so you need to be extra focused in developing all aspects of your riding this year." She nodded to Paris, who was at the head of the line. "Walk around the arena once on a long rein, please, before you go back to the barn."

Honey felt a rush of excitement at the thought of an entire dressage module. She loved the discipline and elegance of advanced schooling. She clicked to Minnie to fall in behind Colorado. Once they had completed a circuit, Honey slowed Minnie so Dylan could catch up.

Her friend looked mutinous. "I need to work on Morello's jumping, not his flatwork."

Honey sensed that now wasn't the best time to defend the virtues of dressage. "We'll still get one lesson a week with Ms Carmichael. Maybe you'll be able to practise your jumping then," was all she could come up with as the horses' hooves clattered on to the yard.

"Maybe." Dylan didn't sound convinced as she dismounted and ran up her stirrups.

Lani came up to them. "You guys, do you think I can persuade Mr Musgrave to do dressage with a few barrels strung around the arena? I'm not sure Colorado will cut it if there's nothing more interesting than letters to aim for."

"I don't think Mr Musgrave will go for that, not even if you offered to paint the letters on the barrels," Honey replied as they walked the horses into the barn.

She led Minnie into her stall and slipped her arms around the mare's neck. "Well, I can't wait to start dressage training with you," she whispered. "You're going to be amazing, I know it."

There was a meeting that evening in the common room to discuss the first social event on the Chestnut Hill calendar. Honey was looking forward to getting to know the seventh-graders.

Lani nudged her. "Hey, isn't that the girl Dylan re-routed?"

Honey looked at the dark-haired girl walking further up the corridor. "I can't say for sure. I didn't get too well acquainted with the back of her head the other day," she whispered back.

Lani giggled.

"Emma, wait up!" Two more seventh-graders ran past Lani and Honey to join the girl. They chattered like a cage of birds as they turned the corner and vanished into the junior common room.

Earlier that day Lynsey, Aggninder, and Dillon, the Adams Student Council reps, had rearranged all of the sofas and chairs to form a large square. "Guys!" Razina waved them over to the sofa that she had bagged along with Wei Lin, Alex, Dylan and Malory.

"I think this is the first time I've gotten to sit on this sofa. It was always occupied by the eighth-graders last year," Honey said as she settled back into the squashy cushions.

"And now it's our turn," Lani said with exaggerated satisfaction.

"Make some space, you guys." The sophomores were last to arrive and were left with the option of squashing up on the sofas or standing.

Two coffee tables in the centre of the square were loaded with chips, cookies and sodas. Honey picked up a bowl of chips and offered it to the seventh-graders who were sitting on the opposite sofa.

"Hi, everyone." Lynsey clapped her hands for attention. As she stood up, Honey saw that she was wearing one of her new outfits. *Miss Sixty?* Whichever of her favourite designers it was, the suede waistcoat, underblouse and skinny jeans fitted Lynsey's figure like they'd been specially tailored. "I'd like to officially welcome the seventh-graders to Adams and confirm that the rumours are true." She paused for dramatic effect. "You've just signed up to the best dorm house on campus." She stopped again while the girls cheered and clapped.

"Go, Adams!" Lani whooped.

Lynsey cleared her throat. "Adams also has a rep for holding the best parties and making the best contributions towards school events." She smiled. "No point in false modesty, right?"

"You just tell it as it is," Tanisha Appleton agreed, and turned to exchange a high five with Sydney Hunt.

"We're aiming to help make this year's Homecoming Dance unforgettable," Lynsey went on.

There were more cheers, and then Aggninder, a popular sophomore, took over. She shook her long dark hair back over her shoulders. "The theme for the dance is Hollywood Fabulous. Tonight's all about brainstorming our dorm's share of the detail. Oh, and invitations are to go out to Saint Kits, but it will be by personal invitation, not to the entire school." She grinned. "Classy and selective's the name of the game!"

Honey swapped a glance with Malory, who was squashed up against her. By the way Malory was blushing, it was clear Honey's friend was already planning on inviting Caleb Smith. At the end of the last term they'd finally become more hit than miss as an official item, although Honey knew that they hadn't seen much of each other during the summer. Caleb had been riding the A circuit with the Cavendish Programme and Malory had been busy with her dad.

"Will you invite Josh?" Lani said in a loud whisper.

Honey felt her own cheeks burn. Inviting him to Chestnut Hill's first social event on their calendar was a great idea. Her stomach twisted with nervous excitement at the thought of getting back in contact with Josh. *I'll drop him an email tomorrow.*

"We have been put in charge of designing invitations and we thought it would be a good idea if all budding Michelangelos who can wield a Crayola with style submit their designs by the end of the week," Aggninder continued. "The winning design will be announced on Monday."

Dylan leaned across Honey and caught Razina by the sleeve. "We should all work on one together."

Good call, Dyl, Honey thought. Razina was a gifted artist. She'd inherited her mother's flair for creativity and often accompanied her mum on trips abroad sourcing new lines for her art gallery.

"Are you coming, Wei Lin?" Lani asked as she stood up. She brushed the crumbs off her jeans.

"Sure." Wei Lin put down her soda on the coffee table.

"I was hoping you and I could work on a design together. We can use my laptop," Patience called over to her roommate.

"Sorry," Wei Lin apologized to Lani. She glanced over at Patience. "Looks like I'm spoken for."

Honey's mind was already whirring with ideas as she

made her way to Razina's room. The invitations would have to be sophisticated but fairly easy to produce. *Maybe we could make them in the form of the Oscar award*, she thought, before discounting the idea as too obvious.

Razina's room had amazing framed photographs of Africa hanging on the walls.

"I love this," Honey enthused, looking at the family group of elephants outlined against a vibrant sunset.

"Thanks, I took it in Kenya," Razina told her. "My mom gave me this amazing zoom digital camera for my birthday."

"Did you take all of the photos?" Malory asked as she and Dylan sat down on Lani's bed.

"Yes, I really got into photography this summer," Razina admitted. She opened her wardrobe and pulled down a large plastic box from the top shelf. "Here," she said, carrying it over to Dylan. "Help yourself and hand it around. Let's do some sketches before we transfer the design on to my computer."

"Wow," Alexandra said when she peered into the box. "Did you raid the entire stock of The Stationery Studio?" She took out a pencil and pad and then handed the box to Honey and Lani who were sitting at the double dressing table.

Honey dipped into the box, which was packed full of sketch pads, coloured card, craft work, paints and colouring pens.

"Are we going to work on our own designs or decide on a theme first?" Malory asked.

"Theme first," Honey suggested.

"I've already got one," Dylan announced. "Drum roll please."

Honey began to tap her pencil against her pad and the other girls quickly joined in.

"Chestnut Hillywood," Dylan declared.

"You are such a kidder." Lani rolled her eyes.

"OK, now for the serious suggestions," Razina said.

"I was serious," Dylan said in an injured tone.

Malory reached over to hug her friend. "Maybe we should go for something a bit more subtle?"

"Since when does Dylan do subtle?" Lani teased and then ducked to avoid the cushion Dylan lobbed at her.

"Why don't we make a pretend DVD case? It could be opened up to show the words of the invite," Alexandra suggested.

"That's a great idea, but anything that needs to be opened is going to take a lot more time to produce." Razina shook her braided hair over her shoulders.

Honey began to write down a list of all the words she associated with Hollywood: *glamour, fame, movies, awards.* She paused and then did a quick sketch of a cinema screen. "We could do a card designed like a movie premiere," Honey mused. She drew a red carpet leading up to the screen.

"That's so cool!" Lani exclaimed. "How about sweeping lights in each corner?"

"I'm loving this," Razina enthused. "We could edge the corners in gold to make it look really glitzy."

Honey nodded. "Let's set out the words of the invite

like screen details outside a cinema." She wrote *Homecoming Dance* in chunky black letters.

"I still don't see why we can't use Chestnut Hillywood," Dylan pretended to grumble as she came over to look at Honey's design. "It's looking good, though."

"Thanks." Honey smiled.

She was totally absorbed in shading in her lettering when the door of the room opened.

"Girls! Didn't you hear the buzzer?" Mrs Herson looked in. "You've got two minutes to get this mess cleared and back to your own rooms. I'll check you're all in bed in exactly ten minutes."

She went to step out of the room and then glanced back over her shoulder. "And don't think that hiding under your duvet fully clothed will escape my radar!"

Honey quickly shaded in the last two letters to finish off the invitation. She held it up so the others could see it. "Ta da!"

Her friends gave a round of applause. "I'll transfer it on to my software package tomorrow," Razina said. "Good job, Honey."

Honey felt a warm glow of pleasure. "Thanks, guys." *Now all I have to do is cross my fingers that the judges will think it's a good job too!*

Chapter Three

"*Non, non, non!*" Mademoiselle Dubois jabbed her fingers against the verbs she'd written out on the whiteboard. "Your accent is *très abominable*! It is obvious that you have not spoken in anything other than English for your entire summer vacation!" Their French teacher was directing her comments at the whole class, but it was Lani's poor use of verbs that had triggered Mademoiselle Dubois' angst. She pointed at Honey. "Felicity! Tell me what you did during your vacation. *En Français, s'il vous plaît!*"

Honey stood up. Mademoiselle Dubois had already threatened everyone with double detention for their lack of effort during her class. *If I mess up, she'll probably make it a week of detention.* Honey's mind raced to work out the correct translation before she spoke.

"Today, if you please." Mademoiselle clicked her tongue with impatience.

Honey began to describe her vacation with her grandparents. She'd been helping Sam to catch up with his French conversation over the summer and the vocabulary was still familiar. "*Je suis heureux d'être de retour à la Colline de Châtaigne*," she finished.

"So, you're happy to be back at Chestnut Hill and looking forward to improving your command of the French language, no doubt." Mademoiselle Dubois raised her eyebrows. But her tone was softer as she turned back to the verbs written out on the whiteboard.

Phew, Honey thought when the buzzer sounded to end the lesson. As she put her textbook into her backpack their French teacher announced, "Thanks to Felicity's efforts, you have escaped double detention. However," she looked around the room, her expression stern, "you will return here after study hall tonight to practise your verbs. I will not waste another lesson on teaching you what you should know perfectly well. Honey, you alone are excused. For the rest of you, I want you to remember that you are in the eighth grade now!"

"It's only the second week into term and I'm already beginning to hate that phrase," Dylan said with a sigh as she reached for her bag. "We didn't know how good we had it last year!"

"I feel bad that I'm the only one not coming back after study hall," Honey confessed.

"No so bad that you'll volunteer to join us, I bet," Lani quipped as they filed into the corridor.

Honey was already planning a catch-up call with Sam later that evening. "You got me!" she admitted.

When her brother asked how she was settling in, she groaned. "You have no idea how lucky you are to be homeschooled. If Saint Kits is anything like Chestnut Hill, then you won't know what's hit you when you start eighth grade."

"Tough day, huh?" Sam responded.

"Like you wouldn't believe," Honey told him. "I only just managed to get out of extra French."

"Ah, so forcing me to listen to your French conversation this summer did some good, then? Did the rest of your class manage to escape?"

"No," Honey told him. "Mademoiselle Dubois totally freaked out and made them go back for extra practice!"

"Even Lani?" Sam asked in a casual tone.

"Especially Lani," Honey said. She was quick to notice the way her brother had singled her friend out. "Maybe you should organize that baseball match with her that you both keep talking about. It might help take her mind off French verbs for a while."

"From what you're saying, she needs her mind on her verbs if she doesn't want to spend the rest of her free time doing extra classes!"

"But you will email her?" Honey pestered.

"If I do then you'll be the second to know," Sam promised.

"Not the first?"

"Not unless you know how to hack into Lani's account." Sam's voice shook with laughter. "Now quit trying to match-make and tell me how the riding's going."

Honey smiled. Her brother knew her so well. Minnie was just about the only thing that could have encouraged her to drop the subject of Sam and Lani! She told him how great it was to be reunited with the beautiful grey mare.

"The last time I heard you talk like this it was about Rocky," Sam said when she finally ran out of superlatives.

Honey pictured the stocky chestnut gelding who'd been her first pony and remembered how she'd always thought she could never love another pony as much. *But I do. Even though Minnie belongs to Patience, I love her as much as if she were mine.* She felt the familiar sad sensation at the thought that Minnie would never belong to her. *At least while she's on loan to Ms Carmichael I can look after her as much as if she were mine.*

"Are you OK? You've gone all quiet on me," Sam asked.

"Sure I am," Honey fibbed. "I just suddenly realized that all I've done is talk about me. Tell me about you. How much are you missing having me around?"

"Well, I'm not missing having to beat you off the TV remote," Sam teased.

They chatted a while longer and when Honey finally hung up, she decided to say goodnight to Minnie. The others would be in French for another twenty minutes yet.

Minnie was looking over her stall door almost as if she knew that Honey was coming. Her ears pricked as soon as Honey walked through the open double doors.

"Hello, beautiful," Honey called. She'd forgotten to bring any treats, but Minnie didn't seem to mind. She was content to rest her head on Honey's shoulder while

39

Honey reached up to scratch under her forelock. Honey closed her eyes. *She makes me feel like I've come home*.

"I swear she's been looking out for you all evening."

Honey had been so wrapped up she hadn't heard Ms Carmichael approach.

"You and Minnie sure have become the best of friends." Ms Carmichael smiled.

Honey felt a rush of pleasure. "Like Malory and Tybalt," she said, thinking of the bond between her friend and the beautiful gelding.

Ms Carmichael nodded. "I feel the same with Quince," she said, mentioning her Connemara/thoroughbred-cross gelding. "It's like we're on the same wavelength. Like we each know what the other is thinking."

Honey nodded. "When Minnie's going really well I feel I don't even need to use my reins and legs and she'll just turn in the direction I want her to."

"Well, I don't think we'll try that in any of my lessons. If you did it everyone would want a go and the thought of Dylan and Morello careering around my arena without reins is enough to give me sleepless nights," Ali Carmichael joked. She patted Minnie's neck. "I'll wish you both goodnight now."

"Goodnight," Honey echoed. She reached up to give Minnie a hug, thinking about what Ms Carmichael had said about the bond they shared. "My soulmate," she whispered.

Lani was stretched out on her bed when Honey got back to their room. She had a cold flannel covering her eyes. "My head hurts," she groaned. "You have no idea how lucky you are to have escaped tonight."

"Luck didn't come into it." Honey laughed. "Coaching Sam all summer did. He says hello, by the way."

Lani took the flannel off her eyes and sat up. She pushed her fingers through her short dark hair. "Did he say anything else?"

"We talked about the baseball game the two of you are supposed to be going to," Honey told her. She sat down at her dressing table and began to unbraid her hair so that it tumbled on to her shoulders.

"Not again." Lani went red.

Honey pulled her comb through her hair. "After he got ill the first time, Sam's favourite phrase became *carpe diem*. Have you heard of it?" She met Lani's eyes in the mirror.

Lani shook her head. "It's not more French, is it?"

"Latin," Honey told her. "It means to seize the day, to make the most of the time you have now." She took a deep breath. "Being ill changed Sam. He was convinced for such a long time that he'd never get well and that he'd never be able to do all the things he'd always wanted to. Now, whenever something comes up that he wants to do, he doesn't like putting it off."

Lani came over to give Honey a hug. "I'll email him tomorrow and set something up for half term. Shall I book three tickets?"

"Much as my brother loves me, I have a feeling he'd really rather I sat this date out," Honey remarked with a knowing smile.

Lani pressed her hands against her cheeks. "I have no idea what you're talking about, Miss Harper."

"Yeah, right," Honey told her as she scooped up her dressing gown and headed for the bathroom. "I believe you, thousands wouldn't!"

Honey chose an apple from the canteen self-service bar. Minnie would enjoy the core as a treat later on. She carried her tray through the crowded cafeteria to the table she always sat at with her friends. It was alongside large windows overlooking the main lawn with its ornate fountain.

"Hey, Honey," Dylan greeted her. "Mmm, that lasagne looks good."

"Hands off!" Honey warned as she sat down. "You can't possibly have room for anything other than that burger."

Dylan's green eyes glinted with mischief. "Is that a challenge?"

"Ssh," Lani interrupted. She jerked her head at the table behind them. "Listen."

Honey, Malory and Dylan tuned in to find out what was so intriguing about the conversation Lynsey and Patience were having.

"His name is Daniel Rivers," Patience was saying. "I swear, Lynsey, he's like the best golf pro ever! Can you believe that Dad's managed to persuade him to come and teach here?"

"It's a bummer that you're not allowed to have private tuition with him," Lynsey said. "That's the only way to make real progress when you're training."

Ouch! That sounded like a major dig at Ms Carmichael's group classes. Honey glanced at Dylan, whose scowl showed she was thinking the same thing.

"I know," Patience sighed. "But I can only get credits if golf is on the curriculum. I just hope there aren't many take-ups for it."

"Well, I don't think many from our grade will want to learn how to play. They wouldn't understand how cool golf is even if Gucci started using a pair of crossed golf clubs as a new logo," Lynsey said.

Honey raised her eyebrows at Dylan.

"Do you know something?" Dylan said in a low voice. "I'm suddenly developing an interest in golf. In fact, I might even wander over to the sports department after lunch and see if they're going to be running a golf module this term."

"You are sooo bad." Lani grinned, shaking her head.

"Come on." Dylan pushed her chair back. "Let's go."

Honey hurriedly ate the last of her lasagne and then caught her friends up. "Are you really going to sign up, Dyl?" she asked as she took a bite of her apple.

Dylan's eyes danced. "Oh yes. Can you imagine the look on Patience's face when she sees that she's sharing her golf tuition with me! Besides," she raised her eyebrows and smiled, looking totally innocent, "my dad would love me to get a decent handicap and join him for a round of golf at his club."

They walked out into the afternoon sunshine. The sports hall was opposite the student centre and they followed the path around to its front entrance.

"I wouldn't mind taking some golf lessons," Honey admitted. "My dad took me on the golf range at his club in Wimbledon before we moved out here. I managed to reach the one-hundred-and-fifty-yard marker a few times."

"How about you guys?" Dylan asked Malory and Lani.

Lani shook her head. "Sorry, I can't take on another sports module. I need to concentrate on my softball."

"And I want to focus on my swimming," Malory said. "Plus, I suck at golf. I tried a game of crazy golf with my dad this summer and I actually managed to lose three balls."

Honey laughed. "Nobody loses balls at crazy golf!"

"Exactly! Could you imagine how bad I'd be at the real thing?" Malory said ruefully.

"Never mind, I'm sure I'll be able to get some of the others to sign up," Dylan said as she pushed open the glass doors leading to the sports hall's tiled reception. "I can't wait to see Patience's face when most of eighth grade turn up to her very first lesson!"

The first golf session was scheduled for Friday on the hockey pitch. Honey, Dylan and Razina walked down to the field, where a small group of girls had assembled.

"I guess this blows out Patience's one-to-one sessions!" Dylan remarked.

Honey recognized Madison Ashcroft from Curie, Samantha Field from Granville and Annabel Levi-Williams from Meyer among the seven girls she counted. Patience and Wei Lin were standing a short distance from the rest of the girls. Patience was taking practice shots at a plastic tee. She was wearing a khaki skort, a combination of a skirt and shorts, which she'd teamed with a high-necked zip golf shirt in striking red tartan. Her hair was pulled back in a ponytail and she had a sun visor over her fringe.

Everyone else was wearing their normal tracksuits, with the exception of Madison Ashcroft, who looked as if she was trying to give Patience a run for her money. Her entire outfit was pale yellow, from her golf cap to her Bermuda shorts. Even her knee-length socks were an identical shade.

As Honey, Dylan and Razina drew near, Patience scowled at them. "I didn't think you were into golf."

"Well, they say you learn a new thing every day," Dylan said brightly.

Suddenly Patience looked straight past them and her face brightened into a broad smile. Honey noticed how well her peach lipgloss went with her summer vacation tan. She followed Patience's gaze and saw a dark-haired man in his early twenties driving across the field in a golf buggy.

"Afternoon, everyone," he called. He pulled up a few metres away and cut the engine.

"Hunk alert," Dylan whispered into Honey's ear.

Honey had to admit that their golf instructor was Hot with a capital H. As he jumped out of the golf buggy it was impossible to miss his laughing green eyes, high cheekbones and tousled black hair.

"Good afternoon, Mr Rivers," Patience said. She walked up to him and held out her hand for him to shake.

"Hey, call me Daniel." Their golf instructor grinned, showing a set of teeth so perfect that Honey wondered if they'd been capped.

Patience's colour rose as she said, "Sure, no problem, *Daniel*."

"Do you think he'd let me call him 'Danny?" Dylan said in a low voice.

Honey and Razina stifled their laughter as they watched Daniel lift a bag of clubs from the back of the buggy.

"I've brought clubs for anyone who doesn't have their own," he explained. "For today's session I'd suggest a nine iron. It's got a shorter shaft than the other irons, so the angle of the blade will bring the ball into the air more easily. For anyone with experience, I'd suggest you choose a three iron, as it hits the greatest distance." He drew out an iron from his bag. "First I'd like to watch each of you hit the ball. One at a time please, so I can check out your basic swing."

Patience pointedly drew a three iron from her bag. "I'm ready. Shall I go first?" She took a couple of practice swings before hitting the ball cleanly off the tee. The ball landed just past the two-hundred-yard marker.

"That's a good start," Daniel encouraged. "Don't forget to keep your left arm straight and to follow the swing through."

"I bet I hit further than anyone else will," Honey overheard Patience mutter as she walked back to Wei Lin.

Dylan was next, and took three swings before she hit the ball. When she finally made contact, the ball scudded off the toe of the club and bounced just a few yards, not even making the fifty-yard marker.

"Daniel!" Patience called before the pro had time to comment on Dylan's shot. "Shouldn't this class be divided into different abilities? I don't see how Dylan and I can be in the same class together. It's quite clear she's never hit a ball in her life."

For once Dylan didn't retort but instead handed her club to Honey. "Go get 'em," she murmured.

Honey carefully measured up the ball and concentrated. Taking a deep breath, she swung the club down at the ball. With a rush of satisfaction, she watched the ball land just short of the one-hundred-and-fifty-yard marker.

"Well done!" Daniel exclaimed. He glanced at Patience. "Maybe we should hold off any decision about dividing the class into abilities until everyone gets a shot at the ball?"

Patience smiled at him but Honey noticed it was more forced than before.

Patience bent her head close to Wei Lin's and whispered something. Wei Lin nodded. When it was her turn to hit the ball she swung ineffectually at it and it bounced just a few yards off the tee.

Was that meant to help prove Patience's point that the class should be divided up? Honey wondered as Wei Lin walked back to Patience.

"Good try," Daniel said tactfully. "Let me

demonstrate the best action for hitting the ball off the tee." He stood over the tee. "Stand with your feet about shoulder-width apart, for now place the ball slightly back from centre, grip the club like this and draw the club back." He kept his head down as he spoke. "It's absolutely crucial to keep your head steady with your eye fixed on the ball; then, allow your body to pivot around. . ." He swung the club into the air and brought it down with a swoosh.

"Wow, that was some hit," Dylan commented as Daniel whacked the ball over the perimeter fence.

"Good shot!" Patience exclaimed.

At the end of the session Daniel called to the girls to form a semi-circle around him. "Well done, everyone," he said warmly. "I'm glad to know that I have some real talent to work with." He paused as the girls gave themselves a round of applause. "I think for now we'll keep you all together." He glanced at Patience. "I know that some of you are more advanced than others, but it's a little early in the day for me to be putting you into groups based on ability." He began collecting his clubs from the girls. "I'll see you all this time next week. Until then, when you get a chance, practise your swing!"

Daniel got into his buggy and drove away up the field, collecting up the yard markers.

"I could really get into this," Dylan said as she took another swing with an imaginary club. "Howzat?"

Honey dissolved into laughter. "You say that when you're playing cricket, not golf."

"Amateur," Patience said scornfully as she walked by with Wei Lin.

"Watch this space," Dylan called after her before winking at Honey. "Can you imagine how Patience will choke if I end up with a golf handicap that's lower than hers by the end of term?"

Honey bit back a grin. Dylan was rarely more motivated than when she was making mischief!

Chapter Four

On Friday, as the girls walked down to the barn for their riding lesson, Honey was surprised to see Patience just ahead of them with Lynsey. "How come Patience is here?"

"She missed her last riding lesson because of a dental appointment. Maybe Ms Carmichael said that she could join our lesson to make up for it?" Malory guessed.

Honey's heart sunk. *That means I won't be riding Minnie today.* She took a deep breath. *I can't begrudge Patience riding her own pony. I'm lucky to get to ride Minnie so much as it is.* But she could feel her excitement at the prospect of a lesson fizzle out.

As soon as they reached the barn, Patience made a beeline for Minnie.

"Honey, Ms Carmichael's put you down to ride Blaze today," Kelly said as she walked by carrying an armful of tack.

Honey looked over at Blaze's stall and noticed that either Kelly or Sarah had already put the pony's saddle and bridle over the wall. "I'll see you guys later," she said to her friends, whose ponies were all further down the aisle.

She tried to swallow down her disappointment as she got Blaze ready. "I'm sorry, it's not your fault," she whispered to Blaze, giving the chestnut a swift hug. Blaze gave her a friendly nudge with his nose. Honey patted him and then finished tacking up quickly so she could have as long a warm up as possible. "We're both going to need to get used to each other," she told Blaze as she led him out of his stall.

Honey found it strange adjusting to Blaze's shorter stride. The gelding was only thirteen hands; Minnie was fourteen two. She tried to sit deep in the saddle and relax into his stride. "We'll get there," she promised as she rode him towards the arena.

Paris Mackenzie was already in the arena riding Whisper, along with Tessa Harding on Soda. Honey rode Blaze in and used her legs on every stride to try to encourage him to extend his stride. Soda's pace was much faster than Blaze's and as Honey heard the palomino come up behind them, she circled Blaze off the track to fall back in behind. But the moment Blaze was turned towards the gate he hung towards it, trying to make a quick exit.

"Come on, Blaze, it's not time to go back to your stable yet," Honey said as she pulled her left rein to get Blaze back on the track. When Blaze continued to nap, Honey gave him a kick with her outside leg. She gave a sigh of relief when the gelding finally gave up his attempt to run out of the arena and followed Soda and Whisper instead.

51

By the end of the warm up session, Honey was feeling flustered. Every time they'd ridden past the entrance she'd had to use all of her energy to keep Blaze moving forward. She tried to think positively. *It's good for me to have experience riding other ponies and seeing what makes them tick.*

Ms Carmichael called to the class. "We're going to be working over a grid today. I know we did a lot of gridwork last term, but riding over a simple series of low fences is a great way of helping to spot and correct faults."

Dylan was first up on Morello. Honey heaved a sigh of relief as Morello approached with his ears pricked and took off at exactly the right spot to clear the first cross pole. There was one loud clunk as Morello knocked a trotting pole, but apart from that, he and Dylan completed the grid without a single knockdown.

Dylan gave Honey a look of relief as she halted alongside her.

"I'd like to see a bit more impulsion next time, but well done, that was a nice ride," Ms Carmichael said. "Paris, you can go next, please."

Whisper was Paris's own pony and the bond between them was clear as the grey mare popped neatly into the grid and trotted over the poles before easily clearing the final cross pole. "Good," Ms Carmichael commented. "That was a nice example of seeing effort put in on flatwork paying off. Whisper was beautifully balanced."

Patience was up next on Minnie. Honey noticed that the mare had clamped down her beautiful thick tail and had both of her ears flat back against her neck. Usually they were pricked forward, apart from the occasional flicker back at the sound of Honey's voice. *She doesn't look happy.* Honey tensed as Patience stood up in her stirrups on the approach to the cross pole and overbalanced as the pony took off. She saved herself from toppling backwards by hanging on to the reins. Minnie was put off by the sharp jab to her mouth and landed awkwardly. She recovered as they rode over the trotting poles but Honey noticed her stride falter as she approached the final jump. Honey's fingers tightened on Blaze's reins as she anticipated another jab to Minnie's mouth. Blaze shifted restlessly. "Sorry, boy," Honey murmured.

Patience gave Minnie a kick and managed to keep her balance this time as they jumped out of the grid. "Never use your reins to steady yourself. Grab a handful of mane if you find yourself in trouble, or else use a neckstrap," Ms Carmichael told her.

Patience halted Minnie without patting the mare for her effort. "I don't need a neckstrap," she argued. "My balance is fine usually, it's just that I've been putting in so much golf practice that my new muscles are hard to get used to when I'm riding."

"And the prize for the worst excuse in the entire history of cop-outs goes to Patience Duvall!" muttered Dylan.

For the rest of the session Honey tried not to watch Patience and Minnie but just gave one hundred per cent to her own riding. She was rewarded by Blaze putting in two scopey jumps on the grid.

"Good work," Ms Carmichael praised her. "I'm sure your legs must feel like they're ready to drop off but it's not often Blaze works that effectively."

Honey felt a glow of pleasure as she took Blaze back to his stall. She sponged away his sweat marks and put his stable sheet on before fetching him a small net of hay. As she passed Minnie's stall she automatically looked over the door. Patience had gone but Minnie still had sweat stains and hadn't been left anything to eat.

Honey felt a surge of exasperation. "I'll be back in a minute," she promised Minnie.

"Are you ready?" Dylan called from the top end of the barn. She was waiting with Malory and Lani.

"I'm still finishing up. You go and I'll catch up with you."

Honey quickly tied up Blaze's haynet and gave him a horse cookie before securing his stall door. Then she hurried back to Minnie, who welcomed her with a low whicker. Honey filled a bucket with water and sponged off Minnie's saddle mark, which was already beginning to dry and harden. Next, Honey drew Minnie's face sponge over her eyes and the mare gave a small sigh. "Does that feel better?" Honey smiled as she wiped around Minnie's nostrils.

Once she was sure Minnie was clean and dry, she buckled on Minnie's stable rug and went to fill a haynet. She had missed recess but it was worth it to know that Minnie was OK. "Because you come first, don't ever doubt it," Honey said as she gave Minnie a hug goodbye. "Even when I'm riding a different pony."

Minnie rested her head on Honey's shoulder. "You're my number one," Honey murmured. "Always."

After brunch on Saturday morning the girls went up to Malory's room to get ready for their trip into Cheney Falls. They had arranged to meet up with Dylan's cousin Nat, Malory's boyfriend Caleb, and Josh.

Honey's stomach had been turning somersaults all morning at the thought of seeing Josh again. She'd really missed him over the last few weeks but now she felt as nervous as if it were a first date! She wondered if Malory was feeling the same, as she hadn't seen Caleb since he'd got back from his tour of the summer A circuit.

"Can someone else do my eyeliner for me? My hands aren't steady enough," Malory panicked.

Honey shot her a sympathetic look and then checked her appearance in Malory's wall mirror for what had to be the tenth time. She had pulled back her hair into a French braid with just a couple of tendrils framing her heart-shaped face. She'd chosen to wear her Calvin Klein jeans with her Ichi slinky jersey halter top. Dylan had loaned her a French Connection faux-fur-trimmed waist jacket, which was a perfect match with Honey's calf-length boots. She hadn't put on any make-up yet but had decided to let Lani do it, since her own hands were feeling just as shaky as Malory's.

"Come on, Honey." Lani patted the bed where she was sitting cross-legged. Honey sat opposite her while she rummaged in her oversized make-up bag. "I'm thinking fall colours – rusts, bronze and a hint of gold," Lani pronounced.

Honey opened her mouth to object. She usually went for subtle pinks to emphasize her fair complexion. Her mother always said her skin type was English rose so she wasn't sure if Lani's colour choice would suit her.

"Steady, Lani. You're supposed to be going for coffeehouse chic, not nightclub glam," Dylan said, doing Malory's eye make up.

Honey's doubts increased but she couldn't look in a mirror because Lani was applying her mascara.

"Ignore my critic; she's just jealous that she doesn't have my artistic talent. Now don't move or you'll end up looking like a panda," Lani warned.

When Lani was finally done, Honey grabbed a mirror. Lani had gone for subtle everywhere except for her eyes. The dramatic shading emphasized their azure colour, making them more expressive than usual. If Lani had gone to town with the rest of the make-up, the effect would have been overkill. But as it was, Honey loved it. "Thanks, Lani," she said.

"No worries," Lani replied.

Dylan had finished Malory's make-up and Honey admired the effect. Malory didn't usually bother with make-up, but when she did, her large blue eyes were almost startling against her pale complexion. She was wearing her black curly hair loose, and with the Inwear navy jersey dress she'd borrowed from Lani and knee-high boots, she looked amazing.

"Caleb's going to be drooling," Honey said. "You look great."

"You too!" Malory's eyes shone.

"I'm beginning to feel like the poor relation," Lani complained. "Maybe I should put on my new Ecko sweatshirt."

"Now come on, Lani, you and I have to occasionally step back and let the others get a little attention." Dylan pretended to be serious.

Lani gave a mock sigh. "You're right. To be honest, it will be nice not to be beating the boys off with a stick for once."

"In your dreams," Malory laughed.

"Come on," Honey said as she snatched up her purse. "We've got a bus to catch!"

At the mall the bus pulled up alongside a familiar red car. "Isn't that Daniel?" Honey asked as they got off the bus. He had his back turned to them as he loaded parcels into the car boot.

"It sure is, although I still can't get used to thinking of him on a first-name basis," Dylan said.

Daniel turned at the sound of their voices. "Hi, girls," he smiled. "Saturday shopping?"

"We may be checking out the golf store," Lani told him. "Everyone's raving about your lessons so much I'm thinking of signing up."

"That would be cool," Daniel enthused, totally missing the fact that she was teasing. "They've got ten per cent off some of their clubs right now. I'd go with you to help you choose but I'm with my girlfriend and I promised her lunch." He glanced down the sidewalk at a tall red-haired woman in her early twenties. She was struggling with an armful of bags from a designer boutique.

"Danny!" she called. "Is there any more room in your car for these? I'll just die if I have to take them back. I've managed to find the most perfect bathing suit with matching sarong, sun hat *and* sandals. It will be perfect for our trip to Barbados."

"I didn't know there were actually people who spoke like that," Dylan murmured to Honey as Daniel hurried over to take the bags.

"Girls, this is Tasha," he introduced. "Tash, these are some of my students."

"I still have no idea why you took the teaching job on," Tasha said, as if the girls weren't standing there. "It's not like you need the money."

Daniel's smile slipped a little. "Not now, Tash. Come on." He placed her bags on the back seat of his open-top car and then held open the passenger door. "Let's go to lunch."

"Can you put the top up? You know I hate the way the wind messes my hair," Tasha said as she flipped down the mirror to check her reflection.

Honey doubted that, since every hair on Tasha's head seemed to be lacquered into place to maintain her expensive-looking feathered bob.

Daniel waved. "I'll catch you later, girls."

"Oh my gosh," Dylan said as soon as they were out of

earshot. "Does his girlfriend have him right where she wants him or what?"

Honey nodded. She was surprised that, with his good looks and success, Daniel was happy for his girlfriend to be calling all the shots.

Inside the coffee shop the girls were lucky to get their favourite booth by the window. Dylan and Lani went to get coffees while Malory and Honey bagged the seats.

"Daniel's not like a normal teacher, is he?" Malory said thoughtfully.

"He didn't pick up on Lani's teasing," Honey agreed. "He's going to be disappointed when he doesn't get a dozen new students on Monday."

Malory giggled. "I wonder why he's taken on the post since he *obviously doesn't need the money.*"

"Do you think she was a model?" Honey mused. "She had to be at least six feet tall."

"Did someone mention a model?" Josh's familiar voice broke in on their conversation. He smiled down at Honey, his blonde hair falling over his forehead. "Hi."

Honey was sure he must be able to hear her heart pounding as he slid into the booth alongside her. "Hi," she said, amazed at how normal her voice sounded.

"Move up," Nat said cheerfully, sliding in alongside them while Caleb settled in by Malory. "Where's my cousin? Off causing trouble?"

"I have no idea why you assume that if I'm not in your direct radar then I must be causing trouble." Dylan arrived in time to hear Nat's comment and began to unload mugs from the tray that Lani was carrying. "In fact, if anyone's earned a reputation in the family I'd say it's you. Remember the time you got caught pouring washing-up liquid into that fountain when we were in Portugal?"

"You've never told us that." Josh laughed as he took his drink.

"After a month of being grounded and my PlayStation being put in the attic, I try real hard to forget," Nat admitted.

Josh turned to Honey. "How's Sam getting on with his home study? Is he still all set to start at Saint Kits after Christmas?"

"I think so." Honey nodded. "I spoke to him a few nights ago and he said he was looking forward to it. Well," she hesitated. "He was until my phone call reminded him that detentions and extra study go with the territory!"

"Guilty as charged." Lani grinned. "Mademoiselle flipped over my accent, which was. . ." She played a mock drum roll on the edge of the table.

"*Très abominable*," the girls chorused right on cue and then burst out laughing.

Josh is so nice, Honey thought. *He's great the way he thinks of other people all the time.* She remembered how well he and Sam had gotten on together during Josh's short stay in England. *It's good that Sam's already got a friend waiting for him when he starts school.*

Malory and Caleb were discussing his success on the A circuit that summer. "Gent was a total star. He picked up two blue rosettes and one red. We only took one fall – a water jump where I got a complete dunking." He paused. "It wasn't the same without you, though," he said. "I hope you'll get selected this year."

"Me too," Malory admitted. "I only got to compete at one show this summer but Tybalt wasn't a bit nervous. By next summer I hope he'll be ready for the A circuit – if I get offered another place, of course."

"Those two will never run out of conversation while they have horses in common!" Josh murmured to Honey.

"Is that an invitation for me to start talking about Minnie?" she teased.

"Absolutely, as long as you don't mind that all I know about horses is that they have four legs, a head and a tail," he joked. He picked up a pack of cookies from the tray to offer round.

Honey relaxed. Being with Josh was so much fun. She had intended to send Josh a Homecoming Dance invitation once they'd been printed but now they were together she had a sudden urge to ask him face to face. She took a deep breath. "We're holding a Homecoming Dance in a fortnight and we're allowed to invite a partner from Saint Kits. Would you like to come?"

Josh's cheeks darkened but he gave her a wide smile. "It sounds great, I'd love to come. Who will you be inviting as your partner, though?"

It took Honey a moment to work out he was teasing her. Feeling her own cheeks burn, she laughed and took a pretend swipe at him.

"Ah, *l'amour*," Lani sighed, clasping her hands to her chest.

"You'd know," Honey shot back. "Isn't there a certain baseball date on the horizon?"

Everyone at the table turned their attention to Lani, who tried to hide behind her hands. "Enough already!"

"How come everyone's getting hooked up apart from me?" Dylan complained. "I might start getting all bitter and twisted if it goes on for much longer!"

"You never know. Daniel Rivers might come to his senses and ditch his girlfriend. You could play off for him against Patience," Lani suggested.

"You don't think for one minute that she'd play fair? She'd attack me instead of the ball!" Dylan did a mime of Patience wielding a golf club.

"Oh, you don't think Patience has a crush on Mr Rivers, do you?" said Malory. "He's the golf pro at Chestnut Hill," she explained to the boys, who were looking mystified.

"Even Patience has more sense than to waste her time falling for one of the faculty," Lani commented. "Anyway, I don't think his girlfriend would allow it."

"You know Patience," said Dylan. "She probably thinks a cute instructor is the latest accessory!"

Chapter Five

Honey pulled Minnie's forelock out from under the browband and dropped a kiss on her nose. "For luck," she told the pony. Today was their first dressage session with Mr Musgrave and Honey couldn't make up her mind if the butterflies in her stomach were down to nerves or excitement. "And I have to warn you that thanks to my session with Blaze, I now have muscles of steel in my legs!"

Minnie gazed at Honey with her beautiful dark eyes, delicately outlined in black. Honey smiled. "I bet you make all the other ponies jealous with your gorgeous looks." She heard the sound of hooves clattering along the aisle as her classmates began to make their way out of the barn. "Time to go," she told the mare.

Once they were out on the main yard, Honey checked her girth before mounting. When she clicked to Minnie, the mare automatically turned towards the indoor arena where they usually had their lessons. Honey guided her in the opposite direction. "We're outside today," she told her. The twin reins of the double bridle felt difficult to arrange through her fingers and hands. All the members of the class were riding in double bridles today. "Sorry, Min," Honey apologized as she tried to shorten both reins at once and ended up dropping the curb rein.

Finally she was ready and rode down to the arena where Mr Musgrave had the class riding circuits. Lynsey and Bluegrass were at the head of the class. Bluegrass had his neck arched and his tail was streaming like a banner as he trotted along. Mr Musgrave waved at Honey to join the class.

Honey joined on the end of the class behind Lani on Colorado. When she used her legs on Minnie to match the pace set by Lynsey, the mare responded by extending her stride. Honey felt a rush of relief.

"Good afternoon," Mr Musgrave said once everyone had arrived. He took off his cap and ran his hand over his short grey hair while he waited for Dylan to nudge Morello back to the group. The paint pony was fidgeting and refusing to stand still. Once Morello was standing back in line, the riding instructor spoke again. "I'm looking forward to working with you this term and I'd like to make a few things clear right from the outset."

"Girl on the grey pony." He pointed to Paris Mackenzie. "Your right stirrup is slightly longer than your left." His clipped English accent reminded Honey of her old life back in Britain.

"You will be working at Second Level this term and I assume that you are familiar with any technical dressage terms I will use. For those of you who are not,

I suggest you collect a printout from Ms Carmichael's office and learn them pronto!"

Oh my goodness, he talks like a textbook!

"I believe that some of you haven't had experience of riding in a double bridle." Mr Musgrave swept his glance over the class. "All of the school's horses are used to double bridles for dressage. The reason we use the double is to help develop a greater degree of lightness. I will be watching you all carefully and *anyone*," he stressed the word, "riding with heavy hands will go back to using a snaffle. The double must be ridden with a light hand! Check that you're holding the reins with the broad snaffle rein under finger three, and your curb rein under finger two." Honey glanced down and was relieved that she was holding the reins correctly. "Hold both reins in place with your thumbs," Mr Musgrave finished. "Only use your curb when it's needed; its weight alone will be putting pressure on the most sensitive parts of the horse's mouth. It's there to encourage the horse to keep its jaw relaxed and its poll flexed."

He turned to look at Lynsey. "Girl on the first pony, ride out to the top of the arena and trot down the centre line towards me."

Honey didn't dare look at Dylan, who was alongside her on Morello. The look on Lynsey's face at being called "girl" and then being asked to do something as basic as ride a straight line was priceless.

"You will be expected to ride simple changes of leg, counter change, travers and walk half pirouette by the end of this module," Mr Musgrave told the class as Lynsey nudged Blue forward. "Next year I would expect you to be working on your half pass, collected walk and full pirouette in walk." He tapped his crop against his leather riding boot. "This module is essential preparation, and failing is not an option."

Lysney had reached the top of the arena and trotted down towards Mr Musgrave. She halted in front of him and raised her eyebrows.

"Your pony's shoulders weren't completely straight," Mr Musgrave informed her. "You ride a little too positively with your left hand and your right leg so the pony is bending to the left and his shoulders are moving a little off the track to the left." He stared hard at Bluegrass. "Your pony?" he asked.

"Yes," Lynsey said, her voice almost as clipped as Mr Musgrave's.

"Thought so," he said. "OK, swap with the girl on the buckskin, please."

Lynsey looked at Lani. "What?"

"Swap," Mr Musgrave repeated. "I'd like to see how you ride when you're off your push-button pony."

Underneath her riding hat, Lynsey's cheeks flushed dark red. "Ms Carmichael has never made me to ride another pony. I don't see the point, seeing as I'll only ever compete on Blue. And if you're suggesting Lani should ride him, I don't want him spoiled by being ridden by somebody else. He's an A-circuit pony!"

"Young lady, it is of no interest to me what your other instructors may or may not have asked you to do.

Furthermore, your pony may be up to the A circuit, but it is my job to make sure that you are, too. I am telling you to ride a different horse. Now, please." Mr Musgrave kept his tone calm.

Out of the corner of her eye, Honey could see Dylan's shoulders tremble with laughter.

Lynsey took her time to quit her stirrups. She brushed her gloved hand over Bluegrass's gleaming dressage saddle before she walked away. *Does she think Lani's going to scratch the leather in the few minutes she's sitting on it?*

"Don't worry, boy, I'll arrange post-trauma counselling," Lani said in a stage whisper as she jumped down from Colorado. She led him over to Lynsey and swapped reins.

Lani mounted Bluegrass and gathered up the reins. Honey noticed her bite her lower lip, and guessed she was feeling pretty nervous.

"I want you to go first." Mr Musgrave pointed to Lani. "Trot down the centre line to A, then trot a twenty-metre circle and transition to walk precisely when you return to A."

Bluegrass's stride was less engaged than usual, but he went forward obediently, and when Lani rode the circle he gave the correct bend. Lani's expression was serious as she concentrated on the movement. When she brought Bluegrass to a halt, her expression cleared and she looked delighted. "He's lovely," she said.

"Good. Much of it was down to the horse you were riding, as it's clear you haven't had a great deal of dressage experience. On the plus side, you have good balance and a strong, straight spine, all excellent starting points. But beware of bending the horse's neck too much to the inside," Mr Musgrave summarized. He turned to Lynsey. "Off you go."

As Honey watched Lynsey ride Colorado through the movement, she couldn't help admire how well she handled the gelding. Colorado was great at flexing but he could be stubborn until he got to know his rider. Honey had expected him to play Lynsey up but she soon had him bending correctly.

"Excellent," Mr Musgrave told her. "You may swap back now." The smug expression on Lynsey's face vanished when Mr Musgrave added, "But don't forget that your outside leg is there to assist your outside hand. And I'd like to have seen your inside hand encouraging a little more flexion."

While Lani and Lynsey readjusted their stirrup leathers, Mr Musgrave addressed the rest of the class. "If you're always riding the same horse you can become complacent, particularly when you're on the type of horse that knows what it's supposed to be doing and is willing to respond to weak signals. It's good every now and then to ride different horses and reassess your own strengths and weaknesses."

Honey thought back to her lesson on Blaze and how hard she'd had to work. She had to admit that Mr Musgrave was right. *But please don't ask me to swap Minnie!* Luckily the instructor seemed to be satisfied that his point was made and didn't ask anyone else to change horses. Instead he turned to Dylan. "Since Morello is clearly bored with standing still, let's give him something to do. I'd like you to ride the same movement as the others just did, please."

Morello tracked left and trotted down the school, carrying his head higher and higher. Dylan backed up her leg aids with her whip and pushed her hands forward to try to get him to lower his head. Morello just shook his head and swung off the track. Dylan put her leg behind the girth to push him back and kept using it firmly so he couldn't run out again. When they reached A, Dylan began to ride the circle. As she asked for a bend with her inside hand Morello threw his head up so far he looked as if he were stargazing.

"He's above the bit and hollowing," Mr Musgrave called. "Half halt and collect, please!"

Dylan grew even redder in the face as Morello fell out of the circle and gave a small buck.

Mr Musgrave tapped his riding crop against his leather boot. "It was my understanding that you were all working to a level above basic flatwork. I'm prepared to give you private flatwork lessons in the place of your general lesson with Ms Carmichael each week until you reach the same level as the rest of the class. Have a think about it and let me know."

Dylan looked flustered and upset as she rode Morello back to the line. "I can't lose my one shot a week at jumping practice," she whispered to Honey. "There's nothing wrong with my flatwork; it's just Morello gets totally bored."

Honey wished she could reach out to hug her friend.

"Moonlight Minuet next, please," Mr Musgrave called.

As Honey rode Minnie down the school, she couldn't throw off the feeling that something wasn't quite right. Morello had never played up like this before. Could this be a sign of something more serious than being bored?

Honey took Minnie's saddle and bridle back to the tack room and began to dismantle the bridle so she could sponge it over. She was unbuckling both sets of reins on the double bridle when Dylan joined her. "Are you OK?" Honey asked sympathetically.

Dylan pulled a face. "I can't believe we're being made to concentrate on dressage in the same term as the team tryouts. I really need to have more jumping sessions to get Morello up to scratch." She sighed. "I'll have to tell Mr Musgrave that I can't take up his offer to swap our general lesson with Ms Carmichael for extra flatwork tuition."

"Guys, you will never, ever guess my news even if you spent until the end of term trying!" Nadia Simon from Granville burst into the room.

Dylan raised her eyebrows at Honey. "What would you say our options are?"

"Er. . ." Honey played along. "Well, I guess we could try guessing while we stand here getting old. . ."

"Or you could just tell us," Dylan finished up.

Paris Mackenzie and Leah Bates, who were saddle-soaping at the far end of the room, looked over.

"Yeah, come on, Nadia, 'fess up," Paris called.

"It's not me who has to confess anything," Nadia said dramatically. "I'm not the one pretending to be something I'm not."

"Huh?" Honey was confused.

Nadia took a deep breath. "I've just seen one of the seventh-graders from Walker."

Honey swapped a bemused look with Dylan. Why was this news?

"And?" Dylan put Morello's saddle on one of the freestanding racks and unhooked the stirrup leathers.

"She's an equestrian celebrity! I saw her picture in this double-page feature in the *Virginia Horse and Rider* a couple of weeks ago. Her surname's Macleod, I think. She's one of the hottest stars on the circuit!"

"Really?" Honey checked. "How come this isn't big news already?"

Paris nodded. "If this was true, we'd know already, Nadia."

"Hang on." Dylan frowned. "Think for a second. Ms Carmichael will know who this girl is. Maybe Aunt Ali doesn't want her to be singled out for star treatment and has told her to keep her real identity secret."

"Exactly." Nadia nodded. "She hasn't even brought her own horse with her, so I totally buy in to the whole secret thing."

"If she is who you say she is then her horse is probably way too valuable to come to Chestnut Hill. It would be a target for theft," Honey mused.

"Hey! That's another reason for this girl wanting to

keep her identity a secret!" Dylan exclaimed. "Maybe she's scared of being kidnapped!"

"So we have a star rider at school." Leah's eyes widened. "I guess that ties up one of the junior-team places. There are only three up for grabs now."

Dylan folded her stirrup leathers over her saddle and walked out of the tack room.

Honey frowned. Where was she going? She'd been about to start cleaning Morello's tack.

Honey followed her friend in time to see her disappearing into Morello's stall. "Dylan?" Honey looked over Morello's door. Her friend had her face pressed to the paint gelding's neck. "What's up?"

She thought for a moment that Dylan was going to blank her but then her friend slowly looked up. Her eyes were red.

Honey drew back the bolt and hurried into the stall. "What's wrong?"

"I know I'm being dumb," Dylan sniffed. "But if I were into conspiracy theories, I'd say there was a major one brewing to keep me off the team."

Honey stepped back to read Dylan's expression. There was no doubting her friend's seriousness; her face had lost all its colour. "I really wanted to get on to the team again," Dylan confessed. "But it looks like I might not even keep my place as reserve. With Morello's bad performances, and now this hotshot rider who's guaranteed a place, my chances are nose-diving to zero."

"Morello will settle down as soon as he has a few jumping practices," Honey pointed out. "And maybe

Nadia's got it all wrong. It doesn't add up that this girl is such a celeb but has been able to keep her identity a total secret."

Dylan's expression brightened. "We could do some digging around to find out."

"You could just ask your aunt straight out if it's true that we've got a top circuit rider trying out for the team," Honey said gently.

Dylan shook her head. "If this girl really is trying to hide her identity, then Aunt Ali wouldn't give anything away."

"True," Honey admitted.

"She might let something slip if we ask the right questions, though," Dylan pondered. "Will you come with me?"

Right then, Honey wanted to do anything she could to help Dylan feel more positive. "OK," she agreed.

Morello had stood like a rock while the two of them had talked. Dylan rubbed the gelding between the eyes. "It's no use pretending to be good and quiet now. The time for that was when I was asking you to do basic dressage!"

They found Ali Carmichael grooming Quince. "Hi," Dylan said, looking over the stable door. "We came to see if you wanted a hand."

"Isn't it your recess?" Ali straightened up and pushed at a strand of hair that had fallen over her face. She patted Quince's shoulder. "Move over, there's a good boy."

Quince obediently stepped away from her hand, making room for her to walk around to his other side.

"Yes," Dylan replied. "But you know how much we like hanging out around the horses."

Ali Carmichael began combing through Quince's grey mane. "Since when did you go changing your allegiance from Morello to Quince?"

Honey could tell she was teasing, but Dylan seemed intent on getting to the bottom of the "Macleod Mystery" as she shifted her weight from one foot to the next.

"We were trying to work out the dorm divisions of the new girls in intermediary riding," Dylan said. She began to pick at a splinter on the stable door. "It's so we can guess the odds of how many Adams girls will make the junior jumping team. But then we thought it would be a lot easier if we came to you and asked you for the names and houses of the new girls."

"Dylan, this has got to go into the top ten list of crazy things you've said. There are no odds involved! If there were five girls from Granville who were better than anyone else then all five girls would make the team. Now no more questions, please. It's nearly the end of recess." Ali Carmichael shooed them away.

"OK, so I still don't know the girl's first name," Dylan said as soon as they were out of earshot. "I guess I could go online later and see if I can get the low-down on her that way."

"You make her sound like Virginia's Most Wanted," Honey giggled.

They headed towards the student centre. "I wish Aunt Ali had given me a chance to get more info out of her," Dylan said.

"If it is all some major conspiracy, then maybe your aunt's been paid off," Honey teased.

"Kidder." Dylan pretended to punch her arm.

Lani and Malory were lying on the lawn catching the last of the afternoon sun.

"Here." Lani tossed them each a bottle of still water. "I thought you might want these."

"Thanks," Honey said. She sat down and unscrewed the cap while Dylan filled the others in on their fruitless chat with Ms Carmichael.

Dylan sat down and hugged her knees to her chest. "Like Paris said, if Nadia's got it right, there are just three team places up for grabs. Combine that with Morello being off form and what do you get? Zilch chance at the tryouts."

"Maybe you could ask for extra jumping practice," Lani suggested. "You and Morello both did so great last year, I can't believe that you don't have a real shot at the team."

Honey nodded. Lani was making sense.

"Morello deserves to be on the team." Dylan picked a blade of grass and shredded it into small pieces. "OK, so he's not performing his best right now, but he's never let me down before and it's not fair that because he's going through a bad patch he might not get on to the team."

"Everyone knows what a star Morello is," Malory said gently.

Dylan sighed. "I'm sorry I'm being so down, guys. It's just that nothing seems to be working out right now. I've got Mr Musgrave offering me extra flatwork sessions because he thinks I can't do basic dressage. I get a detention for French because my conversation isn't up to scratch. And I can't even get my golf up to a decent handicap because Patience is hogging Daniel for every session!"

"Hey, we all got that detention, except for Honey," Lani pointed out.

"And my handicap isn't improving either – you're not the only one suffering Patience overload in golf class," Honey added with a smile.

Dylan didn't respond. Honey swapped a worried glance with Malory and Lani. This wasn't like Dylan at all. *There's no way she'd be put off by some competition from a seventh-grader. Morello being off form is really getting to her.*

"Come on." Lani checked her watch. "We're going to be late for study hall."

As they headed off the lawn, Honey noticed Patience standing alone at the faculty car park's exit, at the back of Old House.

As they drew closer, Honey saw Daniel Rivers climb into his red sports car and reverse out of his space. He accelerated past Patience, who lifted her hand to wave, but Daniel didn't notice. As he roared past with his stereo blaring out Jon Bon Jovi's latest track, Honey saw Patience's face register a flash of disappointment.

Then she noticed that Patience had changed out of

her uniform and was wearing her new Galliano bolero top. That seemed a little dressy for a regular school day. Was she planning to impress everyone at study hall? Or did she have someone else in mind?

Chapter Six

That evening there was a second meeting of Adams students to announce the winning design.

"We are going to be so late," Honey puffed as she and Lani raced out of study hall.

Malory and Dylan ran alongside them. "It's my fault," Dylan apologized. "I made us late for study hall with all my worrying about that seventh-grader."

"You didn't know that Mrs Marshall would make us pay back the time to the last second," Honey said as they skidded to a halt outside the front door. She held it open for everyone to go through.

"I'm sure they won't announce the winner of the invitation design in the first ten minutes of the meeting," Lani said.

When they burst through the door of the junior common room, all of the sofas and armchairs were taken.

"Check out the seventh-graders on *our* sofa!" Dylan exclaimed. "Hey, Abi, throw us some sodas!"

Abigail Loach shook back her long brown hair before

leaning forward to pick up four plastic bottles. She tossed them one by one to Dylan, who handed them out. "Thanks!" Dylan raised her bottle in a salute to Abigail, who smiled in return.

"It looks as if Lynsey's about to make an announcement," Honey said as Lynsey clapped her hands to get some quiet.

Everyone in the room quickly settled down. Honey felt a rush of excitement. *In just under two weeks, I'll get to spend a whole evening dancing with Josh!*

Even though Lynsey knew who had won, she couldn't resist making a production out of pulling the result from an envelope. "The winner is. . ." She paused and gazed around the room. "Honey Harper!"

Razina threw her arms around Honey. "Yay!" The girls had insisted on putting Honey's name on the entry since she had been the one to come up with the design.

Lani put her fingers in her mouth and gave a piercing whistle.

"Go, Honey!" Dylan whooped.

"It was a team effort," Honey said quickly. "Thanks for the thanks, though!"

"So, now all we have to concentrate on is who we're asking and what we're wearing," Dylan said.

"Which is when the real hard work starts," Lani joked.

Honey unscrewed the top off her bottle of soda. *What am I going to wear? Maybe I'll hire a dress, something vintage.*

"Susannah, we're going to head back to our common

room to brainstorm outfits. Are you coming?" Carrie Janes, a sophomore, called out to her twin sister.

"Sure." Susannah got up from her armchair and brushed out the wrinkles in her knee-length skirt.

"Operation Bag Sofa?" Dylan suggested.

"I'm on it." Honey grinned as she threaded her way between two armchairs and sat in the middle of the sofa before anyone else could claim possession. Dylan, Lani and Malory followed more slowly.

"I called Jake and asked him to be my date for the dance." Lynsey's voice carried over from the sofa alongside. "He wanted to know if you'd like him to ask Morgan?"

"If I wanted to ask a boy from Saint Kits, I'd send my own invitation, thanks," Patience replied. "Most of them are so immature, I can't be bothered."

"Since when?" Lynsey demanded. Before Patience could reply, she stood up and walked away. Her lips were set in a tight line.

I'm not surprised she looks mad. It wasn't one of Patience's most tactful comments. Honey took a handful of corn chips and passed the bowl to Dylan, Malory and Lani, who had just joined her. "Now then," she said. "Let's talk party outfits!"

The next morning, as Honey rode down to the outdoor arena for the second dressage lesson of the week, she remembered the strange conversation between Lynsey and Patience. *I don't get why she's not interested in going to the dance in a foursome with Jake's friend.* Honey's stomach twisted with unease. *Please don't say she's planning another move on Caleb.* She'd hoped Patience's interest in Malory's boyfriend had been squashed once and for all once Caleb had seen through her.

She squeezed Minnie through the arena gate and all thoughts of Patience were chased away as she concentrated on warming up. Dylan was just in front on Morello. The gelding was stiff-backed and was carrying his head high. *It's like he's developing a phobia of dressage. He's not even waiting to get bored before playing up.*

"All right, everyone into the centre, please, except for Dylan and Morello. I'd like you to ride an extended trot down the long side of the school," Mr Musgrave called.

Dylan looked tense as Morello began overbending. This time, instead of going above the bit, his nose was tucked in as he tried to avoid contact with Dylan's hands. Honey's heart sunk as Morello ran backwards and then began shaking his head when Dylan tried to drive him back on to the track. "What is with you?" Dylan muttered as she gave and took with her hands to try to get Morello back on the bit.

"Enough, bring him into the line, please," Mr Musgrave called. "I understand that you don't wish to take up my offer of extra practice before the tryouts but I'm afraid I'm going to have to insist on it after the competition."

Dylan flushed red as she halted Morello in between Lani and Honey. "If we went back to just doing jumping practice Morello would be his old self again, I'm sure," she said in a low voice.

"Maybe we can talk to Ms Carmichael about it?" Honey suggested quietly. Poor Dylan, she and Morello had always been such a fantastic team.

"Thanks, Honey. That's a good idea," Dylan whispered. "I'll try to catch her at recess."

Honey went with Dylan to see Ms Carmichael after they had rubbed down the horses. The Director of Riding was filing paperwork in her office. She shut and locked the top drawer of the filing cabinet before going to sit behind her desk. "What can I do for you, girls?"

"It's about Morello," Dylan said. "He's not settling for me in my flatwork lessons. He's OK when I ride him in my general lesson, but as soon as I even ride into the dressage arena, he begins acting up."

"He's a totally different pony whenever Dylan tries to do flatwork," Honey agreed.

Ms Carmichael pressed her fingertips together. "Mr Musgrave mentioned that you're having trouble in his lessons. I meant to watch your class today but something came up." She hesitated. "I know that you're not crazy about the idea of flatwork, Dylan. Could it be that Morello's picking up on your lack of enthusiasm?"

"I hadn't thought of that," Dylan admitted. "It feels like I'm doing everything to get Morello to work for me, but I hadn't thought that because he knows me so well he might be reflecting how much I'd rather be in a jumping session."

Honey squeezed Dylan's hand in a silent gesture of support.

"Emily Page rode him in a jumping class for me yesterday and he was fine," Ms Carmichael told her. "I think that if Morello senses his rider's lack of interest he'll translate that into bad behaviour. He's a clever cookie and he has high expectations of his rider."

"OK. I'll try to feel more positive about dressage. But if I don't get more jumping practice then I might as well forget even trying out for the junior team." Dylan was breathing hard. "Please can Morello and I have jumping sessions with you instead of dressage just until the tryouts? I promise I'll give a hundred per cent to Mr Musgrave's classes after that."

Honey crossed her fingers for her friend, knowing how much this meant to her.

"Dylan, you're following the exact same module as everyone else." Ms Carmichael spoke patiently. "No one will have any advantage when it comes to the tryouts."

"Won't they?" Dylan asked pointedly.

Ms Carmichael looked confused, missing Dylan's reference to the hotshot rider Nadia had told them about. "Ride Morello with genuine dedication and enthusiasm on Thursday and, if he still acts up, I'll try to fit in a private lesson for you on Saturday, OK?" She picked up a pen. "Now if there's nothing else, I have a mountain of paperwork."

Honey thought her friend would be relieved at Ms Carmichael's suggestion, but as they stepped out of the office Dylan's voice was taut. "There's no way I'm going to have enough time to get ready for the tryouts. They're only just over a week away!"

Honey readjusted her grip on the seven iron and swung at the ball. She was concentrating so much on keeping her head still that she forgot to follow its flight.

"That's great, Honey," Daniel enthused, making Honey look up. He ran his hand over his shortly cropped hair. "You're in a good position to get the ball on to the green with your next shot." He pointed to where the ball had landed a couple of hundred yards away on the fairway. "You're a real natural. Don't forget to follow the swing through, though."

Honey felt a buzz of happiness. It was great to be playing on a proper golf course rather than on the school hockey field. Daniel had driven the class to Cheney Falls golf club in the minibus to play nine holes. She retied her hair so it was off her neck, which felt sticky in the late summer heat, as she stepped aside. Patience took her place. She placed her ball in the tee and measured the distance with her eyes half a dozen times before taking her shot. It landed just short of the green.

"I'm still not getting the swing a hundred per cent accurate," she complained.

"You just made a near-perfect swing." Daniel's blue eyes sparkled with enthusiasm. "And I wouldn't say it's ruining your game. You've almost reached the green in one shot! We'll make a pro of you yet!'"

"But I'm not consistent," Patience argued. "I sliced the last shot."

Daniel put his arm around her shoulder and gave it a quick squeeze. "Don't be so hard on yourself! I don't want you to burn out before we're halfway through the term. You're doing much better than you realize."

Patience turned red. As she turned away her golf club dropped from her hand.

Her colour was high as she retrieved her club and stood back in line as Razina walked up to take her shot.

Honey stared at Patience. *Oh my gosh. She's got a crush on Daniel!* Suddenly everything started to make sense: Patience hanging out in her best clothes as the instructor drove by; Patience dismissing the Saint Kits boys as partners for the dance; Patience monopolizing Daniel's attention in their lessons. Honey felt a stab of concern. Surely Patience had to know that this couldn't go anywhere?

That evening, in the common room, Honey was uncomfortably aware of how much Patience was raving about their golf instructor. *How come I didn't notice any of this before?*

"He totally gets how to teach the game. He's a zillion times better than the golf pro my dad hired over the summer. I've learned more in a couple of lessons with Daniel than I did over the entire vacation." Patience kicked her legs up on the sofa to get comfortable.

"Does she ever shut up?" Dylan joined Honey by the coffee machine. "It's starting to sound like she has a total crush on him!"

Honey was about to say she was thinking the same

thing when Dylan went on, "As if he'd look at someone in one of his classes! Trust Patience to think she's so much more mature and sophisticated than the rest of us."

Before Honey could react, Dylan had marched across to Patience. "We saw Daniel at the mall on Saturday," she announced. "It was really nice seeing him and his *girlfriend*."

Honey froze. If her suspicions were right, Patience was in way too deep to handle this sort of blunt information. But Dylan hadn't finished. "She's absolutely stunning. Red hair, long legs, amazing complexion; she has to be a model. It's no surprise that Daniel is smitten with her."

Two spots of bright red appeared on Patience's cheeks. Her fingers were clutching the edges of the cushion on her lap so tightly, the knuckles looked as if they were about to burst through her skin. It seemed as if the common room had gone quiet, but Emma Bachelor and Katherine Unwin were still battling their game of ping pong out and Razina and Alexandra were debating what DVD to put on. No one but Honey seemed to have noticed how shattered Patience was by Dylan's revelation.

She looked at Malory, who was poring over a book on dressage, and jerked her head at the door. She then hurried over to Dylan. "You haven't looked over the finished invitation yet. It's in my dorm room. Come on, I'll show you." Honey took hold of her arm and tugged her away from Patience.

She kept her arm through Dylan's all the way to her room, with Lani and Malory both hurrying behind.

"Do you *really* think Patience has a crush on Daniel Rivers?" Malory asked Dylan.

Dylan glanced over her shoulder. "Totally! But she needs a reality check. As if!"

Honey pushed open the door to her room and clicked on the lights. She headed for the folder on her desk. As she pulled out the invitation, Lani joined her.

"That was pretty harsh. It wasn't so long ago that Dylan was crushing major league on a certain Henri," Lani murmured in Honey's ear. It was a fair point. Last year, Dylan had been constantly bringing the French boy she'd met while skiing in Aspen into their conversations and none of them had even come close to telling her to can it. *Maybe she was just using Patience to let off some steam. She's pretty stressed about the tryouts and Morello's behaviour.*

Honey was saved from having to respond to Lani's comment by a knock at the door. Lynsey looked into the room. "Do you guys mind if I hang out here with you for a while?" Without waiting for an answer she came in and headed toward Honey's dressing table. She picked up the topaz earrings which had been a birthday gift from her parents. Lynsey held them against her ears and tilted her face to admire the effect. "I never thought I'd say it but lately Patience has morphed into such an airhead. I had to escape before I went into meltdown. I can't take hearing one more thing about how much Daniel Rivers rocks."

"So what I said didn't shut her up then?" Dylan groaned.

"Are you kidding? Within minutes she was straight back to how skilled he is and how *amazing* he is to be sharing some of that talent with us when it's so *obvious* he doesn't need this as a job," Lynsey mimicked Patience.

Honey sat down on the bed beside Malory, who was experimenting with different colours of nail varnish on each of her fingernails. "Here, let me do your toes," Malory offered. "Patience always has to have a craze," she mused as Honey pulled off her sock and propped her foot on a cushion. "Remember that term she spent chasing Caleb?"

"And the term she was determined to get on to the junior jumping team with Minnie," Honey added.

Dylan collapsed dramatically on Lani's bed. "So we have months to go of Patience's obsessing? Argh!"

Lynsey turned to face her. "It's worse for me. I'm the one who has to listen to her every recess!"

"I think you'll find it's worse for us," Lani said straight-faced. "We have to put up with Patience's friends crashing into our room."

For a second Lynsey stared at her. Honey wondered if Lani had gone too far, but then Lynsey's lips twitched.

The girls burst into laughter, apart from Dylan, who threw herself backwards on the bed. "You guys, there is no humour in this situation!"

The next morning Lynsey was at her usual table in the canteen. "I guess we're not her new best friends after all," Lani joked to Honey as they helped themselves to blueberry pancakes.

Honey raised her eyebrows. "Was there ever any doubt?"

They walked over to their table, where Malory and Dylan were already eating. As they drew nearer Dylan froze with her fork halfway up to her mouth. She was staring straight past Honey's shoulder.

Honey and Lani put their trays down on the table and turned to see what had grabbed Dylan's attention. Patience and Wei Lin had walked through the canteen doors. *Patience is wearing her golf cap to breakfast? No way!*

"Please don't tell me this means we can expect Lynsey to be joining us for breakfast any time soon." Dylan finished her pancake and tore back the lid of her yoghurt.

"Don't worry, it looks as if she's hanging on in there," Lani said dryly as Lynsey made room on the table so that Patience and Wei Lin could deposit their trays.

"Patience Duvall, take off your hat indoors, please!" Mrs Herson called from the faculty table.

Patience turned red as the noise level in the canteen dropped and everyone turned to look at her. Reluctantly she reached up to pull off her cap and Honey instantly understood why she'd worn it in the first place.

"Someone call 911 and tell the fire service one of their hydrants has escaped," Dylan giggled.

Honey didn't want to stare but she couldn't help it. Patience had dyed her hair a vivid shade of red! British postboxes, Santa's coat, Rudolph's nose, squashed tomatoes – none of these were quite as red as Patience's glowing bob.

"If you were trying to make some sort of fashion statement then I'd say you've achieved your goal." Lynsey's voice carried over the shocked murmurs that had spread around the room. "I'll give you ten out of ten for daring, if nothing else."

Patience shrugged. "Everyone knows that brunette is so last season."

"It's true," Dylan agreed. She reached up to touch her own natural colour, which wasn't nearly as startling as Patience's adopted shade but was still defiantly russet. "Just don't let anyone forget that I set the trend and Patience is only a follower!"

The noise level in the canteen returned but Honey found she'd lost her appetite. She had a sinking feeling as she remembered what had happened in the common room last night, and how Patience had looked when Dylan made her dramatic announcement. Was she the only one making the connection between Dylan's outburst about Daniel's red-haired girlfriend and Patience's new hair colour?

"Come on, Dyl," Lani urged. She tore open her Hershey bar. "Aren't you dying to know what's inside?"

Dylan had just collected a large brown envelope from her mail slot in the dorm. Thanks to email and cell phones, it was quite an event to receive something via snail mail, and the fact that this envelope had Dylan's parents' address on the back made it even more mysterious.

"Can't a girl enjoy a mid-morning snack in peace?" Dylan pretended to grumble.

"No!" the girls chorused.

Honey reached over Dylan to make a grab at her bag. She yanked out the envelope and waved it in the air. "OK, girls, it's guessing time."

"Mr and Mrs Walsh have won the lottery. They're going on a permanent vacation and are sending Dylan details of all the places they're staying at in the first year of their nomadic existence," Malory said teasingly.

"Nah. I think they've finally come to their senses and realized what a financial burden their daughter is. They've sent Dyl her own adoption forms to go find new parents," Lani said, her eyes sparkling with fun.

"Cheers, guys. With friends like you I'll never have an issue with my ego!" Dylan grabbed the envelope out of Honey's hands. "Drum roll, please."

The girls tapped their hands on the picnic table as Dylan ripped open the envelope. She tugged out a sheet of paper and a copy of *Horse and Rider*. As she scanned the piece of paper, her expression turned to disbelief and then excitement. "You guys totally lack any imagination. Your guesses are sooo boring compared with this!"

"Come on, come on, 'fess up," Honey begged.

Dylan flipped to a section of the magazine that was bookmarked. She turned the magazine around to show them a photo of a striking chestnut pony clearing a cross-country jump. "His name is Starlight Express," she told them. "He's up for sale."

"He's lovely," Malory enthused.

Dylan nodded. "I used to ride him at my old riding stables. He jumps anything put in front of him and his paces make you feel like you're floating on air." She looked up. "My parents are offering to buy him for me!"

Malory threw her arms around Dylan. "Congratulations! That is so unreal!"

"Move over!" Honey laughed as she and Lani also tried to hug Dylan.

"Amazing!" Lani exclaimed. "And perfect timing too, with Morello being off colour. You could ride him for the tryouts."

"He sure looks as if he'd give Bluegrass a run for his money," Malory said admiringly. "What breed is he?"

"He's a Dutch Warmblood x Thoroughbred. Rubenstein was his grandsire." There was a note of pride in Dylan's voice as she mentioned the Grand Prix champion.

"Wow!" Lani shook her head. "I think you should do everything you can to get him here in time for the tryouts, Dyl."

"Wait a minute!" Malory exclaimed. "Doesn't that pony look like Minnie?" She jabbed at a photo with her finger.

Honey glanced at the photo Malory was pointing out. "It's like her twin," she agreed, seeing a pale-grey mare with a dished face.

"Here, let me have a look," Lani said, reaching out her hand.

Dylan handed her the magazine.

Lani read the advert. "Oh my gosh." She turned pale and looked at Honey, her eyes wide with horror.

Honey grabbed the magazine and scanned the details of the pony that looked just like Minnie. *Moonlight Minuet, 14.2hh dappled-grey Connemara mare, for sale through no fault of her own. . .*

Honey went cold. "No," she whispered as the magazine fell from her hands. "Please, no."

Chapter Seven

Honey didn't know how she made the walk from the student centre to their maths class. The words of the advert kept spinning around and around in her mind until she thought she would scream. *Minnie was for sale!*

As they walked into the classroom she could feel Lani and Dylan close by. "We're here for you," Dylan whispered as Honey sat down on her chair.

Honey pretended to concentrate but Mrs O'Hara could have been talking in Double Dutch for all she was aware. When they had to do calculations in their exercise books, Honey drew sketches of the most beautiful pony in the world surrounded not by a heart but by a dozen question marks. *Why was she for sale? And why hadn't Patience said anything?*

By the time the bell rang for lunch recess, Honey was ready to burst. Seeing Patience helping herself to a portion of pasta, she walked by the queue and pulled on her sleeve.

"Watch it!" Patience snapped as the serving spoon upended over her tray instead of her bowl.

Honey ignored her protest. "I saw the advert for Minnie. You can't seriously be selling her?"

"Moonlight Minuet is one majorly valuable horse but whenever I ride her she acts like a bargain-basement pony." Patience shrugged. "And it's not as if I'm interested in riding any more. I want to focus on my golf game. You can't give me one good reason to keep her apart from the fact that you like to pretend she's yours."

Honey flinched. Did she pretend Minnie was her own? *No, I'm always one hundred per cent aware that she belongs to Patience, and wishing that she didn't.* Well, it looked as if her wish was about to come true.

"Patience, you are such a drag!"

To Honey's amazement, Lynsey, who was standing in the queue, had jumped in. "You've turned into some sort of golfing nerd. What happened to our plans for you to make the junior jumping team on Minnie by the end of the year?"

"There's more to life than making some dumb school team!" Patience retorted. She threw down the serving spoon and turned on her heel.

Lynsey stepped out of the line and grabbed her arm. "I just don't get you any more! Don't you know what an amazing horse you have? She's guaranteed to get you on to the team – unlike some other ponies on the yard." She looked meaningfully at Dylan. "You're absolutely nuts to let her go."

"Riding is *your* thing," said Patience. "And golf's mine, OK?" She shook Lynsey's arm off and stalked out of the canteen, her scarlet hair swinging.

Honey felt a surge of hopelessness sweep over her. She could see that there was absolutely no point in trying to get Patience to change her mind. It was golf or nothing for her – and that meant no more Minnie.

Honey forced herself to eat a cheese sandwich before heading down to the stables. Sarah and Kelly were bringing in the horses from the fields, preparing for the afternoon classes and were glad of the help when Honey offered to go fetch Minnie.

"Her headcollar's on the hook outside her door," Sarah told her as she led Winter Wonderland into his stall.

Honey walked down the track to the paddocks and scanned the field for Minnie. It wasn't difficult to spot the distinctive grey mare as she grazed alongside Tybalt. "Minnie!" Honey called.

At the sound of her voice, Minnie stopped grazing. She swung her head around and stared in Honey's direction.

"Minnie," Honey called again. As the mare nickered a welcome and began to walk towards her, Honey's throat tightened. It wouldn't be long before Minnie wouldn't be here to answer her call.

When the mare was just a few metres away, Honey held out a horse cookie. Minnie closed the gap and lipped the treat off Honey's palm. "Good girl," Honey told her as she slipped the headcollar over Minnie's nose.

She led Minnie out of the gate and back to the barn,

trying to memorize the way the pony walked, how she gave an occasional friendly nudge with her nose, how she knew which stall was hers and walked straight in. But deep down Honey knew that she didn't need to save anything to memory. She already had the mare committed to her heart.

Honey picked up a body brush and began to clean Minnie's coat. *How can I ever bear to let her go?* As she brushed, she tried to let the rhythmic strokes soothe her. But the words still pounded in her head: *I'll never see her again, I'll never see her again.*

During their dressage lesson it was as if Minnie could sense that Honey needed comforting. When they lined up the mare swung her head around and nibbled at Honey's boot.

"I want you to ride down the length of the school and choose a point to give and take the reins," Mr Musgrave announced. He pointed at Honey. "You go first, Felicity."

Honey rode away from the group and trotted up the centre line. She tracked left and made sure that Minnie was balanced before she gradually released the contact on the reins. Minnie kept trotting with her neck arched and her hindquarters engaged. After a few strides Honey re-took the reins and Minnie's outline still didn't alter. "Good girl," Honey whispered as they reached the end of the school.

Dylan, Malory and Lani clapped harder and longer than anyone else and Honey felt a rush of appreciation for her friends' support.

"Good, good," Mr Musgrave called. "That wasn't just a fine example of the horse's self-carriage, it was also an excellent demonstration of trust between horse and rider. Well done!"

Before today Honey would have felt thrilled at Mr Musgrave's compliment. Right now it was all she could do to stop herself bursting into tears knowing that the bond she and Minnie shared would soon be broken for ever.

Dylan was up next and wasn't feeling at all confident, if the face she pulled as she rode away was anything to go by. Morello laid his ears flat as they turned down the long side of the arena. He was already resisting Dylan's hands and his trot was fast and unbalanced. When Dylan released the reins, Morello dropped his head and his trot became a canter. *It's as if he's trying to run away from her, but that doesn't make any sense; he loves Dylan.*

Honey's heart went out to Dylan as her friend rode back to the class.

Mr Musgrave shook his head. "Young lady, if you are intending to try out for the junior jumping team then I would suggest you seriously consider riding another pony."

Honey felt sick with worry. Things couldn't get any worse for Dylan, with the tryouts just days away.

Honey spent longer than usual rubbing Minnie down. She skipped out her stall, rinsed out her bucket and fetched a fresh salt lick to replace the old one. When she couldn't find anything else to do she leaned over the wall and watched Minnie pull at her haynet.

Honey took a deep breath. Every moment with Minnie from here until the mare was sold would be spent saying goodbye. *And I can't deal with that.* No, today was the last time she would ever come to see the grey mare. Her heart felt as if was breaking as she kissed her fingers and held them out to the pony. Minnie looked at her with trust and affection shining in her dark clear eyes. Honey felt her own eyes begin to burn with tears. "Goodbye, Minnie," she sobbed before she turned and ran up the aisle and out of the barn.

She didn't stop running until she reached the lower yard and knocked on Ms Carmichael's office door.

"Come in," Ali Carmichael called.

Honey pushed open the door and found her instructor typing out an email.

"Honey." Ms Carmichael didn't look surprised at her appearance. "Take a seat."

Honey sat down and blurted out, "Minnie's up for sale."

Ali Carmichael sighed. She flipped down the lid of her laptop and looked at Honey with sympathy. "Yes. Mr Duvall told me a couple of days ago to expect phone calls from prospective buyers. I'm sorry, Honey. I know how much you love Minnie."

Honey felt sick. This was so unfair. Minnie was happy at Chestnut Hill and now she was going to be sent to a new home with a new owner who could never appreciate the mare as much as Honey did. *I have to think positively. I have to believe that Minnie will go to someone who will love her every bit as much as I do.*

"I was wondering if you'd assign me a different horse to ride," Honey said in a rush. "Being with Minnie now is just too hard. . ."

Ms Carmichael sighed. "Honey, I'd love to buy Moonlight Minuet for the school, she'd be such an asset, but I just don't have room in the budget."

"I know." Honey bitterly repeated Patience's words. "She's a very valuable pony."

"In more ways than one," Ms Carmichael said softly.

Honey nodded, not trusting herself to speak. But she had a feeling that Ms Carmichael understood exactly how she felt.

"You can't be serious?" Lani stared at Honey. "You should be spending as much time with Minnie as possible, not keeping away."

Honey shook her head. "I can't, Lani." She rolled over in her bed to pick up the photo of Rocky from her bedside table. "I never thought I'd say this, but losing Minnie is even harder than losing Rocky."

Lani sighed as she switched off her bedside lamp. "I know. But I think you'll end up regretting this. Minnie isn't going to understand why you're suddenly not visiting her each day."

"She'll just have to get used to it," Honey said miserably. "We both will."

It wasn't long before Lani's breathing became deep and regular. Honey stared into darkness and suddenly felt the need to call Sam. Silently she swung her legs off the bed and slipped into the bathroom. She used her cell to call her brother and crossed her fingers that he would have his own phone switched on. To her relief Sam answered in two rings. "Hey, Hon, what's up?"

"I wasn't sure you'd have your phone switched on, or that you'd be awake," Honey confessed.

"I had a feeling you were going to call," Sam said. "I've been worried about you. Are you OK?"

Honey hitched herself up to sit on the double sink unit. "Not really. I found out this morning that Minnie's up for sale."

"Oh, that's terrible. I'm really sorry." Sam sounded upset. "I thought she was on loan to the school?"

"I don't think it was for a specified time," Honey told him. "Mr Duvall was clearly free to take her back whenever he wanted." She closed her eyes. "How do I handle seeing strangers coming to ride her, knowing that one of those strangers will end up taking her away?"

"You're the strongest person I know," Sam replied. "I'll never forget how brave you were when you went through the operation to give me your bone marrow. You kept telling me you were fine right up until the anaesthetic knocked you out." He took a breath. "I know that this is going to hurt like crazy and I know that being told you'll pull through isn't any comfort to you right now so all I'm going to say is that I'm here for you and if you need a shoulder to cry on, you can use mine."

"Thanks, Sam," Honey whispered. "I needed that."

101

"I love you, sis."

"I love you too."

The next day Dylan had an extra Saturday practice session just as Ali Carmichael had promised. When she rode Morello into the ring the paint pony had his ears pricked and was looking relaxed.

"OK," Ms Carmichael said after they had warmed up. "Let's see how he goes."

Honey leaned forward in her seat in the viewing gallery. Lani and Malory had been scheduled for extra practice with softball and swimming and hadn't been able to watch. "Go, Morello!" Honey spoke aloud as the paint gelding cantered up to the first fence, a low cross pole, and flew over it. Morello's stride was rhythmical but lacked impulsion as he took the following seven fences. He took two bricks out of the wall, his heels rattled several poles and he brought down the final combination. *But at least his headshaking has disappeared.*

After the final fence Dylan slowed Morello and patted his neck. "That was better, boy. You just want to be back in the jumping arena, don't you? Am I able to have a few more extra practices like this?" she asked her aunt.

Ms Carmichael shook her head. "Sorry, Dylan. You and Morello have to follow the same curriculum as everyone else. I can't be seen to be giving more to you than any of the other students." She gave Dylan's arm a quick squeeze to take the sting out of her words. "Can you rub down Morello and turn him into the field for me, please?"

Honey hurried down the viewing gallery stairs and around to the yard in time to meet Dylan. "Morello was much more like his old self," she told her friend.

"Definitely." Dylan nodded as she ran up Morello's stirrups. "But he's lost his edge. It's like he hasn't got confidence in me. I was working like mad to get some energy into his pace but it just wasn't happening."

"I know how much you want to ride Morello for the tryouts," Honey said as they walked the pony back to his stall. "But if you can arrange to get Starlight Express brought here by the end of the week, maybe you should think about riding him instead?"

Dylan led Morello into his stall. Instead of beginning to untack him, she pressed her face into his mane. "I feel like I'd be letting Morello down." Her words were muffled. "We're supposed to be a team."

"Yes, but when Starlight arrives, you and he will be a team," Honey said gently. "You and Morello will always have a special bond, but when you have your own pony here then he'll be the one you'll be riding. It wouldn't make sense to buy him if you're not going to give up Morello."

Dylan pulled away from Morello and sighed. "I know. But I can't get my head around the idea of competing on a different pony, even Starlight. And anyway, I don't know if we could get him out here in time for the competition. I just want to get Morello to quit behaving badly during dressage."

Honey watched Morello take a mouthful of hay and suddenly throw up his head.

"Steady," Dylan warned as the pony skittered sideways. "See," she tried to joke. "I've only got to mention the D-word and he's acting crazy."

Honey frowned. She'd seen a pony behave like that before – and it hadn't been out of naughtiness or high spirits. She stepped into the stall with Morello's headcollar. "Can you hold his head for me?"

"Sure. What are you doing?" Dylan asked as she helped to buckle the headcollar.

"I'll let you know in a minute," Honey said. She slipped her fingers into the back of Morello's mouth where he didn't have any teeth. "Come on, boy, open up." As Morello made a snatching action, Honey quickly took hold of his tongue so he couldn't close his mouth. She peered inside. "Look, Dylan!" There was an angry raised weal in his mouth, like a large ulcer. "There was a pony at my old riding stables who had an ulcer like that and his behaviour was exactly the same as Morello's. I didn't make the connection because Morello wasn't playing up during his jumping sessions. It must be the double bridle that's hurting him. With the snaffle sitting higher in his mouth above the curb bit, I'd guess it's rubbing against the ulcer. Poor boy!"

Dylan looked stricken. "I was so convinced that Morello was bored at dressage. What does that say about my relationship with him, that I didn't realize he was in pain?"

"Don't beat yourself up over it," Honey said. "It really

looked like he was just misbehaving. At least we know what's wrong now." Honey unbuckled Morello's headcollar. "If we tell Ms Carmichael she can call a vet to get the ulcer treated. And since he's OK being ridden in a regular snaffle, then I'm sure it won't be long before his confidence comes back. A few sessions of being ridden without any pain and I bet you'll have the old Morello back."

Dylan nodded and managed a smile. "Which means we should be OK for the tryouts."

Honey hugged her. "And I'll be there cheering you on!"

Chapter Eight

On Monday Honey rode Blaze for the dressage lesson. She was relieved to be on the dark-chestnut gelding, who would need her entire concentration to produce any results. She wouldn't have time to think of how much she was missing riding Minnie.

"Wish me luck," Dylan said as Mr Musgrave called her to ride.

"You don't need it," Honey said loyally.

Being ridden in a snaffle made all the difference to Morello. Ms Carmichael had called the vet as soon as Dylan and Honey had gone to her with their discovery. The vet had started him on a course of antibiotics and agreed that riding Morello in a broad eggbutt snaffle wouldn't interfere with the abscess.

Honey watched the gelding trot down the length of the school as Dylan gave and took her reins. His pace didn't alter and he remained totally balanced. *Great!* Morello gave a loud snort when they'd finished the movement and when the class burst into applause, the paint gelding half bucked in a playful response. Dylan's face was flushed. "Good boy," she said, patting his neck. "Good boy!"

"Well done, Dylan. It's good to see you and Morello back on form." Mr Musgrave congratulated them.

"Thank you," Dylan mouthed to Honey and gave her the thumbs-up sign.

Honey smiled, and tried to ignore the jolt of sadness at the thought of Minnie's empty stall being filled by a new pony. She was determined to concentrate on how much fun it would be getting to know Starlight Express. Her fingers tightened on the reins. *I won't think about Minnie leaving. I won't.*

Honey and Razina were in charge of collecting all of the responses to the invitations that had been sent out so the numbers could be accurately catered for.

"Rachel Goodhart has asked if we'd design a banner to go over the gym door," Razina told Honey as they counted through the pile of responses. "She thought we could copy the design of the invitations. What do you think? With the dance being on Thursday, it means we'd only have tomorrow and Wednesday to get it done."

"I think we could do it," Honey said.

"Great," Razina enthused. "Rachel says she's checked with Mr Woolley and he's going to clear us a space in the art room to work in."

Honey was just relieved to think that her free time would be taken up with preparations for the dance. Right now she couldn't think of anything worse than having time on her hands to struggle with the longing to visit a certain beautiful grey mare.

"Hey, Honey." Malory walked into the art classroom. "We were thinking of going for a trail ride. Do you want to come?" There were no lessons that Thursday afternoon so the school could prepare for the dance.

Honey looked up from the poster that she and Razina were putting the finishing touches on. "Sorry, but I've promised to put this up at the gym. Have a great ride. I'll see you later."

Malory looked disappointed and opened her mouth as if she was going to argue. Then she gave a small shrug. "Later."

Honey watched Malory walk out of the room and longed to run after her. She could tack up Minnie and they could canter over fallen tree logs. Later they would walk on the woodland tracks over a carpet of gold and bronze leaves. *No, it's better this way.* She turned back to the poster and forced a bright smile on her face. "How about we go and put this work of art up for everyone to admire?"

"Sure." Razina began to roll the banner up. "Although you do know that if we go within a five-metre radius of the gym we'll be roped into helping out with everything else?"

"Suits me," Honey said.

They made their way over to the gym, which had both sets of double doors propped open. Once Honey and Razina had attached the banner over the door with the help of a borrowed stepladder, they wandered into the gym. It was hard to believe that the chaos inside was going to be fully sorted in five hours' time. Chloe Bates, who was vice president of the school, and Mrs Herson were directing the placement of chairs and small tables around the walls. A senior, Katharine Arnold, had paused while rolling a red runner down the length of the gym to allow one of the maintenance staff to fix a huge silver glitterball to the ceiling.

Lynsey hurried up to Honey and Razina, carrying a clipboard. "We need all of the tables at the back covered in gold tablecloths. You'll find red runners in one of the boxes on the stage to lay down the middle of each table."

"OK," Razina said. She looked around. "Isn't Patience helping out?"

Lynsey rolled her eyes. "She's arranged for her own stylist to spend the afternoon getting her ready at Cheney Falls' salon! Talk about over the top!"

Honey hid a grin. Lynsey was usually the centre of attention at Chestnut Hill's social occasions, with her seeming limitless access to the latest designer fashions. She wouldn't be pleased at the thought of having Patience attempt to rival her.

Lynsey tapped her pen against her clipboard and got back to the subject of preparation. "Could you then go over to Domestic Science? Mrs Brightwell is loaning cutlery and plates that all need to go on the first of the tables. We're expecting a delivery of table decorations and plastic glasses, which need to be put out as well." She took a breath.

"How about we do all that and then get back to you?" Honey said quickly. The way Lynsey was going, they wouldn't be left with any time to get dressed for the party.

"Well, OK, just don't forget," Lynsey called after them. "We're going to need all the help we can get if this party is going to be another Chestnut Hill success!"

Honey had downloaded a picture of Marilyn Monroe the day before and pinned it above her dressing-table mirror. With the theme of Hollywood Fabulous, she'd decided to go vintage with one of the most famous screen icons of all time.

Her hair felt uncomfortable wrapped up in curlers and she reached up self-consciously to feel the prickle of the rollers against her fingers. She wasn't going to put her make-up on until she was dressed and, because she'd made an early start, she had time to help the others, who had come in late from their ride.

Malory dashed into the room. "Lani, I can't find the Fendi shoes you loaned me!"

"Chill." Lani was carefully sticking on false eyelashes. "You put them on top of your wardrobe to keep them safe."

"I've already looked, they're not there." Malory sounded alarmed.

"I'll come help you," Honey offered. She followed Malory out of the room and quickly located the sandals on her wardrobe shelf.

"I remember now. I moved them so they wouldn't

get a layer of dust. Thanks, Honey." Malory gave her friend a quick hug before she darted into the bathroom.

"Honey! I look like an orange on a stick!" Dylan panicked. She had changed her usual foundation by one shade to go for a Julia Roberts look but it had left a distinct line of colour on her jaw.

"No worries. Here, let me help," Honey offered. She sat beside Dylan and smoothed small amounts of foundation from her jaw down her neck, carefully fading it into Dylan's natural skin tone. "OK, you're all set to go."

Dylan smiled. "That's twice this week I owe you."

"No worries," Honey said cheerfully. "Now, if my work is done here, I've got a white dress to squeeze into."

"Mission accomplished?" Lani asked when Honey went back to their room.

Honey nodded. "Wow! You look hot."

Lani twirled. She had decided not to mimic any of the Hollywood stars, but with her hair sculpted against her face and her BCBG Max Azria beaded empire dress, she oozed twenty-first century glamour.

Lani zipped Honey into her dress and then helped her to apply her make-up. "Minimal except for the eyes and lips," she decreed as she carefully outlined Honey's lips with liner. She then gently pulled out the curlers and applied a light spray of hair lacquer.

Honey had bought a scarlet-red lipstick especially for that night, but when she painted it on she wondered if it was too much.

"Are you kidding? You're more Monroe than Monroe." Lani caught hold of her shoulders and marched her up to the full-length mirror.

Honey stared at her reflection. She hardly recognized herself with curly blonde hair and full lips. Her white dress tucked in at her waist and then flared out. "You don't think Josh will think it's too full on?" she fretted.

"Josh is going to love it," Lani said firmly. "Come on. Don't forget we're supposed to be meeting in the foyer for a group photo."

Honey grabbed her purse before switching off the light.

Down in the foyer most of the Adams girls had already assembled. Mrs Herson was trying to fit them into the frame of the camera as they chatted and laughed. "Come on, girls, give me your best smiles. Let's have everyone say that no one does Hollywood glamour like Adams House," she encouraged. Each of the dorm houses were going to have their photos published in the school newsletter.

"Can't you put it on timer so you can be in the picture too?" called out Christabel Snowdon, the Adams representative for the newsletter. The girls responded by whistling and clapping. Mrs Herson had made herself up as Audrey Hepburn and, with her hair swept up into a chignon and her pearls and oyster-coloured ball gown, she looked the epitome of chic.

With a laugh, Mrs Herson balanced the camera on the end of the banister. She hurried back to join the girls and within a couple of seconds the flash went off.

The girls gave a cheer and quickly broke up to head over to the gym. As they walked across campus, Honey admired Razina's Halle Berry look. "I thought about wearing my two-piece swimsuit and doing the whole James Bond thing but this won out." Razina smoothed her hands over the soft folds of her Donna Karan black wrap and tie dress.

Malory, like Lani, had chosen not to do a take of any particular Hollywood star, but Honey couldn't help noticing a resemblance to Courteney Cox. She wore a simple strapless sheath which, almost unbelievably, she'd made as a project in Domestic Science out of cappuccino-coloured silk. "Remind me to commission you to make my next party dress," Honey said with admiration.

"It turned out OK, didn't it?" Malory said as she gave the dress a self-conscious tug.

Dylan had opted for a long red dress which didn't look as if it was giving her much room to move in. She'd bought it because of its similarity to one Julia Roberts had worn in one of her old movie roles. *But Julia Roberts hadn't been about to go party with a couple of hundred school friends!*

"Total wow factor, but I don't know how you're going to entertain us with one of your crazy dance routines," Honey remarked.

Dylan winked. "Ah, for that I have a cunning plan."

Up ahead, the Saint Kits bus was parked at the side of the road next to the gym. Honey felt her heart race as she searched the crowd for Josh's familiar blond hair.

113

"He's up by the doors with Caleb," Lani murmured in her ear.

Honey saw Josh, Nat and Caleb waiting beside the entrance to the gym. They all looked incredibly cute in their black tuxedos. Josh broke into a wide smile and waved when he saw them. Honey squeezed Malory's arm. Tonight was going to be so much fun!

Josh joined her as they queued to walk through the doors. "I almost didn't recognize you," he murmured. "I don't think you've ever looked as stunning as you do tonight."

Honey glanced at him, wondering if she'd heard right. Josh was looking ahead, his cheekbones tinged with a blush. But as Honey looked away she felt Josh reach for her hand and happiness surged through her.

The gym looked very different from its earlier chaos. A lighting gantry had gone up over the dance floor and multicoloured lights illuminated the darkened hall. A band had set up on the stage and the lead singer was belting out the latest Avril Lavigne track.

"Oh, cool, check it out." Dylan nudged Honey and pointed at the wall behind the buffet table. Movie stills of some of Hollywood's most famous leading men and women were being flashed up.

"Should I get us a drink?" Josh raised his voice above the music.

"If you boys get the drinks we'll go get a table, they're filling up fast," Dylan suggested. She led the way over to one of the few empty tables. On the next table Mr Woolley, Ms Hutson and Daniel Rivers were already tucking into food from the buffet. Daniel was the only person at the dance to be wearing a white tuxedo but Honey had to admit that he looked fabulous in it.

The boys arrived with a tray of drinks and a bowl of chips, which they set down alongside the mock Oscar candle holder. "You girls sure know how to throw a party," Caleb commented as he took his seat alongside Malory.

"And you have dramatic entrances pretty much tied up too," Nat added. He was staring at the doors.

Patience was standing there, framed in the lamplight from outside. Her red hair had been toned down and was swept up behind a pearl tiara. She wore a strapless full-length ball gown of champagne-coloured silk with a fishtail hemline. Even her jewellery was perfect. She wore a matching diamond pendant and earrings and full-length black silk gloves.

"How come I suddenly feel underdressed?" Lani muttered as Patience headed into the room.

She walked so close to Daniel Rivers' table that Honey thought for one moment that she was going to sit on the spare seat. Patience paused and looked deliberately at Daniel before moving on to Wei Lin and Lynsey's table. Lynsey stood up to let Patience through and for once her Cameron Diaz look, courtesy of a short glittering Prada jersey dress and bangs cut into her blonde hair, didn't stand up to Patience's full-on glamour.

Honey and Josh went to the buffet table, and as Honey selected some chicken salad, Patience joined them. Honey noticed that further up the table, Daniel Rivers was loading his plate with jerk chicken and rice. Had Patience come over just because he was there? Lynsey and Patience were famous for refusing to eat at these events in case they spilled food on their gowns. As Patience poured herself a soda, the liquid almost sloshed from the glass because of how much her hand was trembling. Honey felt a rush of sympathy. It looked like Patience's crush on her golf instructor was starting to take over her life.

She took her plate back to her table and as they were eating the band began to play Ne-Yo, "Because of You".

"This is my favourite!" Honey exclaimed.

"Is that an invitation to dance?" Josh teased.

"Definitely." Honey jumped up and grabbed Josh's hand. Caleb and Malory followed.

Dylan joined them after a few minutes with Eleanor Dixon's brother, Kevin. Honey giggled as her friend bent down to tug at a hidden zip and her long overskirt fell away to reveal a shorter, looser skirt. "I told you I had a cunning plan," she reminded Honey as she twirled around.

"Leave it to Dylan to pull some tacky stunt to try and get attention," Lynsey said, her voice loaded with distaste as she walked by with Jake and Wei Lin.

Honey noticed that Patience didn't dance at all. Instead she was sitting alone, her back ramrod straight in the beautiful dress. *Is she going to spend the whole evening sitting alongside Daniel's table?*

The band finished playing and Chloe Bates stepped

up to the microphone. "Hey everyone, I hope you're having a good night. Does Chestnut Hill know how to party or does Chestnut Hill know how to party?" Everyone in the hall raised the roof with a deafening cheer. Chloe waited until the noise dropped and then held up an envelope. "I've got the winning numbers from the raffle here. Good luck, everyone!" She tore open the envelope and pulled out the card. "Third prize, a gift voucher for Amazon, goes to ticket number 52."

Everyone clapped as Alice Sykes, one of the seventh-graders in Curie, went up to the stage to collect her prize.

"Second prize, a ticket to Kings Dominion Theme Park, goes to number 128."

After Heidi Johnson from Potter had collected her envelope, Chloe turned to the band. "Could I have a drum roll, please?"

The drummer began to softly beat his sticks, building up into a crescendo, as Chloe announced, "Tonight's first prize is an amazing offer of a private golf lesson from our very own professional, Daniel Rivers. Mr Rivers is going to present the voucher, which he assures me can be redeemed at any time!"

Daniel walked up to the stage and was given the details of the winning ticket by Chloe.

Honey sneaked a glance at Patience, who was staring intently at Daniel. She clutched a wad of raffle tickets in her hands.

"Number 297!" Daniel called out.

Patience's expression froze as Julia Gard, one of the

seniors, went up to collect her voucher. She didn't join in the clapping but continued to stare as Daniel shook the senior's hand. He leaned forward to say something to Julia, who laughed.

"OK, everyone, enjoy the rest of your evening!" Chloe called, handing the mike back to the band's lead singer.

As Daniel followed Julia off the stage, Patience walked purposefully through the crowd. She reached Daniel just as he took the last step down on to the dance floor. Honey slipped her hand into Josh's, suddenly feeling anxious, though she couldn't say exactly why.

"Are you OK?" he asked, his green eyes reflecting concern.

Honey shook her head.

Dylan came to stand by them. "She's setting herself up for a fall."

Josh looked confused. "Who?"

"Patience." Honey's throat was dry.

They were close enough to hear every word.

Patience smiled up at Daniel. "Will you dance this next one with me?"

A look of surprise passed over the golf instructor's face. "That's really nice of you to ask, Patience, but I think I'm needed at the back of the hall to make sure there's not a riot when the potato salad runs out!"

Honey had to give it to Mr Rivers; he'd let Patience down tactfully. The beat of the next song began to fill the hall and Patience's response was drowned by the music.

As Honey began dancing again, she realized Patience

was looking utterly devastated. All of her colour had drained away as she pressed her hand against her mouth and pushed through the crowd towards the door. Dylan was dancing with Kevin, Lani and Nat. They were mirroring each other's moves as they worked to the beat. Honey continued to dance with Josh but she couldn't match the others' enthusiasm. *I should go see if Patience is OK.* She noticed Daniel making his way out of the hall. Had he realized that Patience was upset? Was he going to speak to her? On the other hand, Daniel might just be going to check on the potato salad situation. Which meant Patience could be outside alone and feeling miserable.

"I need to go check on Patience," Honey told Josh.

"Sure. Do you want me to go with you?" he offered.

"Thanks, but I think this is a girl thing," Honey told him.

A look of relief passed over Josh's face. "Just holler if you need any boy backup." He paused and then winked. "I'll make sure to send Kevin and Nat out!"

Honey gave Josh's arm a quick squeeze before she threaded her way through the dancers and out of the main doors. It was dark outside but she could see Patience a short distance away. She was sitting on a bench under one of the ornate Victorian lamp posts that lined the campus paths.

Honey hurried past other partygoers who had come outside for fresh air.

"Hey, Honey, where's the fire?" Tessa Harding called after her.

Honey slowed as she approached Patience. The bench was angled away and so she couldn't see Patience's face. *Will she be angry or upset at Daniel's turndown?* Honey hesitated, unsure whether to walk around and sit alongside Patience or call out to her so she could judge if her intrusion was welcome. But as she deliberated, she suddenly noticed that standing a little way off, just outside the pool of light, was Mr Rivers.

Honey heard Daniel speaking in a low voice and felt a rush of relief that the golf instructor had come to sort things out. *I guess I can leave them to it.*

She turned to head back to the hall when Patience's voice split the air. "You can't leave! You were hired for the entire year!"

Honey spun around to see Patience jump up and place her hand on Daniel's sleeve.

Honey stared. Patience was so overstepping the line. She bit her lip, uncomfortable at staying to eavesdrop but burning with curiosity to find out why Daniel was leaving Chestnut Hill.

"I've worked so hard to improve my handicap and now you're going to wreck it all." Patience sounded close to tears.

"You've certainly been one of my hardest-working students this term. It's something I've typed up in the notes I'm leaving for whoever fills my place," Daniel agreed. "And you mustn't worry about your handicap. I'm convinced that you'll continue to bring it down, you're improving all the time."

"But why are you leaving?" Patience asked. She sank

back down on the bench. "Don't you like it here?" She tipped her head back. "Don't you like me?"

"I'm proud of all my students," Daniel replied evenly. "And I'm sure you'll all be happy to know that the only reason I'm moving on is because of fantastic personal news." He paused. "I asked my girlfriend to marry me last weekend and she said yes."

Honey took in a sharp breath. This was the last thing Patience would want to hear.

"I'm afraid I'm not going to be able to give my full commitment to teaching with the amount of preparations Tasha is already proposing," Daniel's voice was humorous. A split second later he sounded baffled. "Patience?"

Patience was on her feet and running along the path as fast as her evening dress and high heels would allow.

Honey hurried up to Daniel. The instructor was staring after Patience, a deep frown creasing his forehead. "Shall I go after Patience and make sure she's OK?" Honey offered.

Daniel looked relieved. "That would be great. Thanks, Honey. Um, Patience seems a little upset at the news that I'm leaving. Can you assure her that the school will be looking to get a replacement for me as soon as possible?"

Honey nodded. *Thank goodness, he's choosing to believe Patience's reaction is all to do with her golf development.*

Patience took the left-hand fork in the path ahead, which led past the student centre and wound around to

Adams. Honey followed her up the stairs and down the corridor to Patience's room. Patience's door slammed a moment before the sound of muffled sobbing came from the room. Honey took a deep breath before pushing open the door.

Patience was hunched up on the bed. She sat up as Honey walked in and dabbed her eyes with a tissue.

"Oh, Patience," Honey said sympathetically, sitting down beside her. "I'm really sorry."

Patience drew in a long shaky breath. "I bet you think I'm pretty stupid getting so hyper just because Daniel rejected me?" She gave a short laugh. "I just hate knowing that everyone heard me make a total fool of myself."

Honey blinked. It sounded like Patience was talking about Daniel turning down her request for a dance. Why hadn't she mentioned the fact that she had just found out the golf pro was leaving? Honey decided to go along with Patience. She was sure the girl would talk about what had happened outside the hall when she was ready.

Honey put her arm around Patience. "I only heard because I was nearby when you asked him. And you didn't make a fool of yourself. It was only a dance. It's no big deal."

"No, but it's a big deal when you get turned down," Patience replied, twisting the tissue in her hands.

"Listen," Honey said. "I'm going to fix up your hair and then we're going to walk back to the hall together. I'm willing to bet no one will stare when you walk back in!"

"Yeah?" Patience considered. "After all the money I paid out today on a personal stylist, they'd better."

"You go, girl," Honey laughed, hugely relieved that Patience was getting a grip.

"But since I can't whip up a personal stylist, you'll have to do with the Honey Harper School of Makeover."

Patience pressed her fingertips under her red-rimmed eyes. "Sounds fine by me."

Honey picked up Patience's make-up brushes from her dressing table. As she drew out an eyeshadow brush she puzzled over Patience's mood swing. *Why hasn't she admitted that she's upset because Daniel's leaving?*

Chapter Nine

"You guys will never guess what Kathryn MacIntyre just told me!" Malory set her tray down on the picnic table outside the student cafeteria. It was afternoon recess and the girls were about to enjoy cappuccinos and brownies out on the patio.

"Well, we could either spend the whole of recess trying to guess, or you could just tell us so we can spend the time gossiping about the news instead," Lani replied, her eyes twinkling.

"It's about Patience and Mr Rivers. I still can't believe it." Malory shook her head.

Honey reached for her drink. Did this mean that Patience had decided to tell everyone that Daniel was getting engaged and leaving? Honey had kept quiet about it all day. If she had spread the news that Daniel was leaving then Patience would have known her conversation outside the gym had been overheard.

"Patience says that Mr Rivers told her last night that he has feelings for her." Malory's eyes widened.

Honey's hand jerked and she sloshed her cappuccino

down the side of its glass. She stared at Malory. "What did you say?"

"Apparently he told Patience that because nothing can ever happen between them, he's leaving the school."

"As if," Dylan snorted.

"The girl is totally delusional," Lani agreed.

"Why would she be saying it if it's not true?" Malory said, her brows drawn in worry.

"Since when did common sense get in the way of Patience grabbing the limelight?" Lani said dryly.

Honey jumped up. She had to find Patience and discover what she was playing at. "I'll be back in a minute," she told the others. "I'm going to get some napkins."

Honey hurried towards the cafeteria and Patience's usual table. Through the crowd of girls gathered around, Honey could see Lynsey sitting on one side of Patience and Wei Lin on the other. Patience was dabbing her eyes with a tissue. Honey frowned. *I've been here and got the T-shirt*. The scene was all too similar to the one she'd been part of the night before.

"I can't believe Daniel's leaving." Madison Ashcroft looked more upset that the golf pro was ending his contract than anything else.

"Don't you mean you can't believe you've been taught for the last few weeks by a total creep?" Lynsey snapped. "We're just lucky he didn't make a pass at Patience last night."

Honey had heard enough. "Can I have a word with you, Patience?"

Patience looked up. "Later," she said.

"Now." Honey could tell that Patience was reluctant to step out of the spotlight. "I've got your evening purse. I picked it up after you left it on the bench last night." She waited for her unspoken message to sink in that she had been outside when Daniel had told Patience he was getting engaged.

Patience narrowed her eyes. "Where is it?"

"In my room," Honey told her.

Lynsey clicked her tongue in annoyance. "I think it can wait. Patience is in shock. She needs to be with her friends." She slipped her arm through Patience's.

"It's OK, I'll go get it and take it back to my room," Patience said, standing up. "I'll be back in a few minutes." She took a few steps forward and then looked back over her shoulder. "I'm trusting you guys to keep what I told you to yourselves, OK?"

The girls nodded solemnly. *And just about every one of them is a first-class gossip,* Honey thought as she walked away. Out of the corner of her eye she saw Nadia Simon from Curie scoot across the canteen and sit down alongside girls from her own. They closed in together and there were no prizes for guessing what they were talking about.

Honey led the way out of the student centre and across the lawn so they could talk in private. Just before they reached the fountain, Patience broke the silence. "Since the Jimmy Choo purse I had last night is back in its box in my wardrobe, why don't you tell me what this little stunt is all about?"

Honey turned to face her. "No, that's my line. I heard every word Daniel said to you last night. He's leaving because he's getting engaged, not because of any feelings he has for you. I'd say this is all a total joke but I can't find one atom of humour in it." She shook her head. "Why are you making up such a total lie?"

Patience shrugged. "I bet Daniel does like me more than the others, though. I could tell we had a connection right from the start."

Honey was speechless. There was a sincerity in Patience's brown eyes that made Honey wonder if the girl actually believed her own lie. "Daniel didn't tell you that," she said. "But you're spreading it around campus that he did. You can't do that, Patience. Daniel doesn't deserve it."

"I only told a few friends and asked them not to say anything," Patience said defensively.

"Telling it to Nadia is like putting it down on an email and copying in every single student in the entire school," Honey said in exasperation.

"Back off, Honey. You don't exactly win a Nice Person Award either. Since when was it OK to listen to a private conversation?" Patience cried. Her eyes flashed with anger. "And when you came after me you pretended you hadn't heard a thing!"

Honey sighed. Patience was beyond reasoning with. "Either you tell everyone that Daniel is leaving the school because he's getting engaged, or I will," she said quietly.

Patience swung her hair back from her face. "You

always act like you're above everyone else, you know that? You're such a drag, Honey!"

"Tell them," Honey said again and folded her arms. Her heart was racing. She wasn't enjoying this confrontation one bit.

Patience's lips tightened into a thin line. She turned to head away from Honey and then spun back on her heel. "You know, with Daniel leaving, I've got a sudden urge to focus on my riding again. Maybe I shouldn't sell Moonlight Minuet. It would be such a shame if something happened to upset me. It might make me think I should get rid of her after all." She flashed Honey a false smile. "Catch you later."

Honey remained rooted to the spot. Patience was blackmailing her! What she wanted to do was race over to Old House and use the PA system to announce that Patience Duvall was a first class liar. But if she kept quiet, Patience would let Minnie stay at Chestnut Hill. Honey couldn't believe anyone would use a pony to protect their lie, but she figured she should stop being surprised by what Patience did. She had what she had been wishing for – a chance to keep Minnie on the yard – but the price was letting Patience spread lies about Mr Rivers.

Recess was nearly over but Honey couldn't face going back to her friends and acting like everything was normal. *I need to get things straight in my own head.* Numbly she walked down to the stable block.

Quince looked over his door at the sound of Honey's footsteps. He was eating a mouthful of hay, and as Honey pressed her cheek against his, she was soothed by the rhythmic munching of his jaws. She tangled her fingers in the gelding's mane and closed her eyes. *If I go along with Patience, I won't have to say goodbye to Minnie. Things can go back to the way they were.* "If I hadn't overheard them speaking last night then I wouldn't know anything anyway," she murmured. *But I did hear them.* She sighed. How much harm could a couple of false rumours do? Daniel was leaving and would never know what Patience had said and within a couple of days everything would have died down. *But the big difference is, if I keep silent, Minnie will be here to stay.*

That night Honey dreamed that Patience was cantering Minnie away from her and no matter how hard Honey chased, she couldn't catch up. When she finally cornered them, it wasn't Patience at all; it was Daniel, who told Honey that he owned Minnie now.

Honey felt woolly-headed and troubled when the alarm woke her. How was she going to concentrate on her lessons? Their first class was maths, and Honey unpacked her books still lost in thought.

"I heard from Madison Ashcroft at breakfast that Daniel Rivers has left! She saw him clearing out his office," Paris Mackenzie announced as she walked into the classroom. "What do you think is going on?"

"You must be the only person not to know," Chantal Lafayette said scornfully.

"Here." Nadia Simon threw a paper aeroplane through the air.

Paris picked it up and straightened it out on her desk.

"OK girls, this looks like major goss. Someone had better tell me what's going on!" She held up the crumpled picture of Daniel and Patience. Daniel had his arm around Patience's shoulders and they were both laughing into the camera.

If you looked closely, it was easy to see that the picture had been tampered with so that the face of whoever had been in the original photo had been swapped with Patience's. Had Patience done this? Honey's stomach churned. This was getting way out of hand.

Dylan took the picture from Paris and screwed it up. She tossed it in the bin. "Best place for rubbish," she said as she walked back up the aisle.

Lani held out her hand to give Dylan a high five.

Everyone piped down as the classroom door opened and Mrs O'Hara came in. She was carrying a stack of papers, which she put down on her desk and began to sort through.

"Honey," Patience whispered from the other side of the aisle. She held out a note.

Honey's stomach churned as she took the note. *My dad's taken lots of calls from people interested in Minnie. I'm still wondering whether I should sell her. What do you think?* Honey stared at the paper until the words blurred. She would move heaven and earth to have Minnie stay at Chestnut Hill and Patience knew it. *But this is all wrong. I have to tell Patience that I'm going to tell everyone the truth.*

Several times that day Honey had thought about approaching Patience, but each time her throat had turned dry and the words had refused to come. Now it was evening and the girls had an extra riding practice scheduled. Honey hadn't planned on going, since she wasn't riding in the competition.

"Come and watch," Dylan urged. "You can practise your Adams House cheer." She shook two imaginary pom-poms in the air. "Go, Adams!"

Honey attempted a smile. She knew her friends were worried about her. They thought that her unhappiness was totally centred on Minnie being up for sale. Honey longed to confide in them, but she knew what their reactions would be. *They would tell me to spread the word about what's really going on. And they're right. I should. But it feels such a betrayal of Minnie.*

As Honey walked with Lani, Malory and Dylan towards the yard, she noticed a small group of people in the outside arena. A grey pony was trotting across the diagonal. Honey reached out and gripped Lani's arm.

Lani glanced at her. "Is something wrong?"

"Someone's trying out Minnie," Honey whispered.

Lani immediately put her arm around her.

Malory looked stricken. "Do you want to go a different way?"

Honey shook her head. "Come on." She prayed that she wouldn't be sick.

As Minnie trotted by, Honey couldn't help glancing at the girl riding her. She was professionally turned out with immaculate cream jodhpurs, polished leather boots, gloves and a navy body protector. She held a light contact with Minnie, who had her neck arched and her tail kinked, looking every bit the dream pony.

"Take her over the jump, honey," the man watching her called. Honey started, thinking for one crazy moment that he was talking to her.

The girl turned Minnie at the jump and Honey willed her to knock it down. *If you carry on behaving so well they'll be sure to buy you. Knock it down, Minnie.*

But Minnie pricked her ears when she saw the jump and flew over it.

The man and woman, who Honey guessed were the girl's parents, clapped. "We're looking to have her as Chelsea's reserve pony," Honey heard the woman say to Aiden Phillips, who was the showjumping specialist at Chestnut Hill. "She's had a fantastic season on the A circuit but we're afraid that if her own pony picks up an injury she'd have nothing to compete on while he recovers."

"Minnie would make Chelsea a wonderful dressage pony, but she can't be overworked. She strained her tendons last year," Ms Phillips explained.

Honey couldn't hear Chelsea's mom's reply. She tightened her fingers against her palms. Minnie deserved to go to someone who would love her, not to an impersonal home where she was just wanted as a spare. Honey was sure that if Chelsea bought her, Minnie would have the best of care. But Minnie was such a people pony, she needed to be treasured as a friend, not just a competition machine.

Dylan gave Honey a hug. "Are you OK?"

Honey nodded, not trusting herself to speak. The truth was, right now she couldn't remember what OK felt like.

Honey watched from the viewing gallery as the class trotted around the ring, but she couldn't concentrate on anything other than Minnie. What would she do when the mare was sold? If Chelsea decided to buy her, would they take her away tonight? Honey felt a surge of panic. She could stop this right now if she promised Patience that she'd keep quiet. Her mind whirled with memories of Minnie: the day the beautiful mare arrived at Chestnut Hill and trustingly walked down the ramp of the horsebox and into Honey's life; the time Honey had nursed Minnie's tendon injury and had given her heart to the gentle, long-suffering pony; the time the pony seemed to give her own heart in return when Honey had started riding her, gaining her trust after she had been worked too hard in the sand school. Honey felt her eyes burn and blinked back the tears which were blurring her vision. She got up. She had to get out of here.

"Whoa, Morello!"

Honey looked over her shoulder and gasped.

Dylan was riding Morello at the second jump on the course, but the paint gelding seemed out of control. He was cantering at the jump side-on, his muscles bunched up. He shook his head violently and then spun around and gave a half rear.

Dylan leaned forward on his neck.

Ms Carmichael ran over and grabbed Morello's reins to keep him on the ground. "Get off!"

Dylan quit her stirrups and jumped down. "What's wrong with him? I thought he was OK in a snaffle!"

Ms Carmichael was checking Morello's mouth. "No wonder he reacted like that. The abscess has spread. The antibiotics haven't worked fast enough, I'm afraid."

Honey leaned over the balcony so she could hear the instructor better. "I'm sorry, Dylan, but there's no way you can ride Morello at the tryouts tomorrow."

Chapter Ten

Honey went down to the yard early the next morning. She tugged up the zip on her jacket against the cold damp air and took the path that led to Ms Carmichael's office. All of the horses being ridden for the tryouts had been left in for the night so they were fully rested. A handsome palomino called out to Honey from the stable block.

"Hey, Soda." Honey stopped to scratch the gelding's nose. The fifteen-three-hands-high horse had been assigned to Dylan for the tryouts. "You've got a big day ahead of you, but do me a favour, OK? Take care of Dylan."

Soda gave a heavy sigh when he realized that Honey wasn't going to feed him. "Don't worry, Kelly or Sarah will be here to serve up breakfast soon," Honey told him. She knew that Dylan was still in with a fighting chance on Soda, since the gelding had a jump like a stag. *But they don't have the bond she shares with Morello.* Honey gave Soda one last pat and went to find Ms Carmichael. She was hoping her riding instructor would be able to help out with an idea that had occurred to her when she'd woken up.

Ms Carmichael wasn't in her office and Honey finally tracked her down in the indoor arena. She was overseeing the building of the course for that afternoon's competition.

A member of the maintenance staff drove past on a quad bike pulling a trailer packed with fence fillers. Half of the course was already constructed, and as Honey looked at the first jump, an upright, she felt a tug of regret that she wasn't competing. *But the only horse I would have wanted to compete on is Minnie.* Her chest tightened again at the thought of being parted from the beautiful mare, and when Ms Carmichael came over to see what she wanted, Honey couldn't help blurting out, "Has Minnie been sold?"

Ms Carmichael ran her hand through her short brown hair. "We received an offer on her last night," she said. She reached out and squeezed Honey's arm. "I know how difficult this is for you."

Honey couldn't speak. She felt sick. She could stop this now if she just promised Patience not to say anything.

"I don't know yet if Mr Duvall is accepting the offer," Ms Carmichael added.

Honey nodded but she knew that even if the offer wasn't accepted, it wouldn't be long before Minnie was sold. *Can I do it? Can I stay silent and let Patience get away with lying about Mr Rivers so Minnie and I can be together?* Honey hugged her arms around herself and tried to concentrate on the real reason she had come to find her riding instructor. "Ms Carmichael, can I run something by you?"

Honey was late for breakfast and the others were finishing up by the time she joined them. She had decided not to share the news about the offer on Minnie. She was still torn over whether she should come clean over Patience's lie and she didn't want anything to upset her friends as they prepared for the competition. *Plus, Dylan's got enough to cope with at the moment knowing that she's not riding Morello.* Honey felt a wave of concern when she sat down opposite Dylan. Her friend's colour was like chalk, and instead of tucking into her usual big breakfast, she had a small bowl of fruit salad.

"I did an Internet search on the Macleod girl last night," Dylan said. "I found an archive magazine on her which described her as one of the most promising young riders to come out of Virginia."

"Come on, Dyl," Honey encouraged. "You need to focus on your own performance, not anyone else's."

"Yeah, on a horse I've never ridden before," Dylan said gloomily. She pulled a face. "Sorry, Honey. I'm just down on myself at the moment. You're right, I shouldn't be stressing about how everyone else is going to do."

Lynsey called over from the table alongside. "Actually, I think you got it right in the first place, Dylan. If this Macleod girl is as hot as everyone is saying, then that's her place guaranteed. My place is in the bag – if I can pick up a fistful of firsts on the A circuit then a junior team tryout will be a walk in the park. That only leaves two places and the reserve. If I were you, I'd save myself the embarrassment of guaranteed failure."

"Ignore her, she's just doing it to get a rise out of you," Lani said in a low voice. "Soda's got a great jump and you're getting to practise on him after breakfast, so he's not going to be a totally unfamiliar ride this afternoon."

Malory nodded. "And you're forgetting what a great rider you are. You're the one who gets the best performance out of Morello."

Dylan pushed her half-eaten fruit salad to one side. "My practice is booked for twenty minutes' time. Will you guys come and watch?"

Honey's heart flipped a somersault at the thought of going anywhere near Minnie. But she knew how much Dylan needed her support. "Of course we will." She spoke for them all.

The girls were quiet as they made their way down to the stable block. Malory was looking a little pale, and although Lani seemed the least affected by nerves, even she wasn't coming up with her usual wisecracks. Normally, as the only one not competing, Honey would be doing all she could to keep her friends' spirits high, but she was so wracked with misery about Minnie that she just couldn't find the words.

Dylan went to tack up Soda whilst the others waited in the outdoor arena. Four practice jumps had been set up to minimize the wait the competitors would have before getting their turn. Dylan was getting exclusive use of them that morning because of her special circumstances.

Honey was surprised when Dylan rode down without their riding instructor.

"Ms Carmichael told me to come down and start warming up. She'll be down in a few minutes," Dylan said as Honey held the gate open for her to ride through.

Ms Carmichael still hadn't arrived after ten minutes. Dylan had Soda cantering in a good outline, and Honey admired the gelding's powerful stride. Dylan set Soda at one of the practice jumps, but Honey could see that their timing wasn't quite right. Soda took off too soon and knocked the pole with his back legs.

Honey felt her heart sink. While there was no doubt that Dylan was a great rider and Soda had a fantastic jump, they needed longer to get to know each other than just one practice session.

Soda was distracted as he took the second jump and rattled it with his heels. The moment he landed, he lifted his head and gave a shrill whinny. There was an answering neigh, and Honey spun around to see Ms Carmichael leading Morello down to the ring.

"What's going on?" Lani sounded confused.

Honey didn't have a chance to reply as she ran to open the gate for Ms Carmichael to lead Morello into the ring.

Dylan trotted up on Soda. "Why's Morello here?" Her eyes lit up. "Has his abscess cleared?"

Ms Carmichael shook her head. "No." She glanced at Honey. "Didn't you tell Dylan your idea?"

"I didn't want to raise her hopes in case you couldn't find one," Honey replied.

Malory and Lani joined them. "He's wearing a hackamore!" Malory exclaimed, fingering Morello's bridle. Instead of a bit, it had a thicker noseband than usual, padded with fleece, with metal pieces extending down from either side. The reins were attached to these, rather than the rings of a bit.

"Will someone tell me what's going on?" Dylan demanded as she got off Soda and handed his reins to Lani.

For the first time that morning Honey felt her spirits rise. "Remember the pony at my old riding school I told you about? The one with an abscess?"

Dylan nodded.

"Well," Honey continued, "his owner got around the problem of his sore mouth by buying a bitless bridle, or hackamore. So I thought that if we could get hold of one you might still have a chance to compete on Morello."

"We didn't have one here," Ms Carmichael put in. "But I did some phoning around and managed to locate one at Alice Allbright's. They couriered it over quarter of an hour ago. All you have to do is to try him out and see how he goes in it."

Dylan's colour rose. She stared at Morello in disbelief.

"I know the idea of riding him without a bit sounds weird, but the bridle works by applying pressure to his face, nose and chin rather than his mouth." Ms Carmichael pointed to the padded nosepiece. "He won't drop his head as much as he does in a bit, but you can still ask him to be balanced and to use his hindquarters. If neither you nor Morello are happy with it, you've always got Soda to fall back on."

Speechlessly Dylan mounted Morello. Honey crossed her fingers behind her back. Not every horse adjusted to a bitless bridle straight away, and it was asking a lot to expect Morello to be ready for the competition this afternoon. But anything had to be worth a try, for Morello's sake as well as Dylan's. The gelding was a little unbalanced to begin with, but Dylan was patient with him. She gave strong signals with her legs and seat and after a few circuits of the arena at trot, Honey could see that Morello was drawing confidence from Dylan's support.

"Try cantering!" Ms Carmichael called.

Dylan pushed the pony forward and Honey let out a sigh of relief as Morello kept his outline and remained totally balanced.

"Take him over a jump," Ms Carmichael suggested.

One, two, three, Honey counted Morello's strides as he bounced towards the upright. His head was a little higher than usual – Dylan was sensibly letting him have his head rather than distracting him with unfamiliar pressure on his nose – but he kept his hindquarters under him and cleared the pole with an enormous leap.

Malory and Honey hugged each other while Lani gave a cheer.

Dylan took Morello over the rest of the practice jumps and, apart from rattling a pole, the gelding cleared them all. Dylan whooped with joy and threw her arms around Morello's neck. When she sat up again, her face looked very red and her eyes were suspiciously shiny. She trotted up to where the others were waiting and jumped down. "I don't know how to thank you, Honey," she said, her voice husky.

As Honey shook her head, too happy to speak, Dylan hugged her over the fence. "I can't tell you how much it means having Morello to ride in the tryouts."

Honey hugged her back. She did know what it meant. *It's how I would feel if Patience changed her mind about selling Minnie. So what do I do?*

"Will you hold Morello for me? I have to see this girl's star potential." Dylan gave Honey the reins. Despite her elation at being reunited with Morello, she was still anxious at what she believed was going to be a guaranteed team place for the Macleod girl. She had ridden up from the practice arena just to watch the seventh-grader's performance.

Alice Sykes, Curie, riding Falcon, four faults, one minute thirty. Now riding, Alyssa Macleod, Walker, on Gandalf, the loudspeaker announced.

Honey understood that Dylan needed to study the opposition, but she wished that her friend would have more confidence in her own ability. Alyssa Macleod trotted into the ring looking immaculate – and, Honey had to admit, totally professional in her tailored navy

142

jacket and spotless white breeches. Even though she was petite, she seemed totally unfazed to be riding Gandalf, who, at sixteen-one hands, was one of the biggest horses at Chestnut Hill.

Dylan joined Ms Carmichael at the entrance of the arena to watch Alyssa's performance while Honey took charge of Morello. She took him down to the lower section of the yard, where Jennifer Quinn, a seventh-grader from Adams, was walking Bella around in circles.

"Nervous?" Honey asked sympathetically.

Jennifer nodded. "I'm up next."

Honey followed behind Jennifer and Bella until the loudspeaker announced, *Alyssa Macleod, Walker, on Gandalf, ten faults, one minute thirty one; now riding, Jennifer Quinn, Adams, on Bella.*

Honey thought she must have heard wrong. There was no way the hotshot rider that Dylan had described would have picked up ten faults in the first stage of the competition.

Honey led Morello back up the yard as Dylan rushed towards them. "Did you hear how Alyssa did?"

Honey nodded. "What happened?"

Dylan tightened Morello's girth. "She started off without any impulsion and brought down the upright and then knocked a brick out of the wall. She approached the double on the wrong leg. Gandalf just about crashed his way through!" She dropped her voice. "Not exactly the hot performance we were expecting."

Honey turned at the sound of hooves clattering on to

143

the yard. Malory and Lani had finished their practice session and were coming up to wait for their turn to jump. Honey would have waved but she was distracted by seeing Alyssa crossing the yard wearing jeans and a T-shirt. She must have changed out of her riding clothes at warp speed.

"Wow, that was quick! What's your secret?" Honey called.

"I'm sorry?" Alyssa looked at her and frowned.

"Your supersonic change," Honey said.

Alyssa's frown deepened.

A shout came from behind them. "Hey, Sienna. Sorry you made the journey from Allbright's just to see me totally bum out!"

Honey turned to see a girl in a navy jacket and white breeches was running out of the barn. *Alyssa?*

"It wasn't your finest hour!" replied the other Alyssa. The girls hugged each other, then the casually dressed Alyssa stepped back and looked serious. "It didn't help that you were over-horsed, which meant you weren't able to use your legs as effectively as I'd have liked. Plus, you didn't do anything to help get your horse out of trouble. You were more like a passenger than a partner. If you'd gotten him on to the right leg, you might not have picked up the second four faults."

Riding-outfit Alyssa held up her hands in mock surrender. "Whoa, information overload! You can draw me a diagram later."

Dylan nudged Honey. "Are you thinking what I'm thinking?"

Honey nodded and dropped her voice. "Twins! And it's not Alyssa Macleod who's the hotshot rider, it's her sister."

Dylan called over to the girls. "Did you happen to make the team at your school?"

Alyssa laughed and answered for her sister. "Of course she did. Don't you know who she is?"

"We do now," Honey said. She caught Dylan's eye and winked, knowing they were thinking the exact same thing: if it was Alyssa's twin Sienna who was the hotshot rider, and she went to Allbright's, Dylan wouldn't have to compete against her for a place on the Chestnut Hill jumping team!

"Hi, I'm Sienna Macleod." Alyssa's sister walked over and introduced herself. "You guys must be pretty nervous right now."

"Just a bit," Dylan nodded. "I'm up next."

"Well, good luck. Watch the distance between the first and second fence. It's deceptively tight and you'll need to watch his stride." She patted Morello's neck. "I know you'll have already paced it out but you'll be amazed at how many people are picking up faults on fence two." Honey exchanged a glance with Dylan over Morello's mane. Sienna was super-confident when it came to giving out riding advice! But then, so would they be if they were tipped for the next Olympics when they were still in seventh grade.

"Do you want a quick tour of the yard before you go back to watch the jumping?" Alyssa asked her sister.

"Sure." Sienna nodded. "Good luck, guys." She

included Lani and Malory, who had halted Tybalt and Colorado a few feet away.

"So that clears up our Macleod Mystery," Honey said as soon as Alyssa and Sienna were out of earshot. "She seemed really nice."

"Yeah, but not so nice that I'd want her competing against me," Dylan replied.

Jennifer Quinn, Adams, on Bella, two faults, one minute nineteen; now riding, Dylan Walsh, Adams, on Morello, the loudspeaker announced as Jennifer rode out of the arena with a clatter of hooves.

"Well, now there's a space on the team, maybe you'd like to go out there and win it?" Honey suggested with a smile.

"Good luck, Dyl," Malory and Lani called.

"Thanks, you guys." Dylan took a deep breath and leaned forward to pat Morello's neck. "Even if we don't get our place, I'll never regret riding you today, my friend."

"Dylan, they're about to announce you again!" Ms Carmichael hurried over carrying a clipboard. "Come on!"

"This is all down to you, Honey. I'll never forget it," Dylan called as she rode Morello towards the entrance.

"There's just one thing I want you to do for me in return: ride the round of your lives!" Honey called back. She joined Ms Carmichael and watched Dylan push Morello into a steady canter without a single headshake.

Morello crossed the electronic line and pricked his ears as he approached the upright. Suddenly he stumbled, his front legs buckling. Dylan was thrown forward on to the pony's neck. Morello was less than a stride from the fence and it looked as if he was going to crash into the poles. Honey gasped, seeing Dylan's hopes of a place on the team ending before they'd begun. But Morello gathered himself up and put in a terrific jump almost from a standstill. His front hooves rattled the bar but it stayed in place and he landed clear. Dylan pushed herself back into the saddle and with a quick pat on Morello's shoulder to thank him for getting them out of trouble, she set him at the second fence. Morello put in a short stride to clear the wall and went on to clear the next four fences. But when he had to jump the stile straight out of a corner, he hesitated. This had always been tricky for him because he tended to flatten his stride on the turn. Dylan sat deep and rode him with determination and was rewarded by Morello's hind legs coming powerfully underneath him. He took off too soon but he had given such a tremendous leap that he just cleared the flimsy-looking rail.

When he approached the final combination, Honey held her breath. Dylan sat still as the gelding launched over the first fence and put in one bounce stride to sail over the final obstacle. The crowd burst into cheers as the announcement came over the loudspeaker: *Dylan Walsh, Adams, clear round on Morello, one minute eleven; now riding, Malory O'Neil, Adams, on Tybalt*.

As Dylan trotted out of the arena she dropped her reins to hug Morello with both arms wrapped around his neck.

Ms Carmichael smiled. "Goodness knows what she'd do if she ever made team captain. She'd probably turn a somersault in the saddle."

Honey laughed and hurried after Morello. As Malory rode by, she and Dylan exchanged a high five.

Honey gave a thumbs-up signal. "I'll be back to cheer you on in a second!" she called to Malory. She dashed over to Dylan as she dismounted, then gave her friend a hug. "You were both amazing!"

"Did you see the way Morello saved us at the first fence?" Dylan's eyes shone. "He's a total star."

Kelly came over. "Let me cool Morello off so you can watch Malory."

"Thanks," Dylan said. She gave Morello a final pat and ran back to the entrance with Honey. Malory had already jumped the first three fences clear. Honey admired her quiet riding style as she encouraged Tybalt to put in a short stride at the spread. She and Tybalt didn't have any of the showiness of Lynsey and Bluegrass, and approached each fence in an understated style that belied their skill and talent. When Tybalt cleared the final fence, Ms Carmichael clapped along with everyone else and commented, "It's starting to look like there's going to be a strong Adams representation on the junior jumping team this year."

Honey swapped an excited look with Dylan before going to congratulate Malory. They passed Lynsey as she rode into the arena. "Good luck," Honey told her.

Lynsey looked scornful. "Luck has nothing to do with

it. It's all about talent and preparation, apart from the occasional performance which can be a total fluke." She glanced pointedly at Dylan before pushing Bluegrass into a trot.

"Someone should tell her to draw back her claws," Dylan joked, not at all fazed by Lynsey's cattiness. But as Honey glanced after Lynsey, she noticed the troubled expression on Ali Carmichael's face. It was clear that the Director of Riding had heard every word.

Lani was walking Colorado at the bottom end of the yard but rode up when she saw her friends come out of the arena. "How's Team Adams doing?"

"Malory and Dylan have gone clear and Lynsey's just gone in to polish her captain's badge now," Honey declared.

"That's brilliant. Well done, guys." For once, Lani didn't give a caustic response about Lynsey. She'd only just missed out on a place on the team last year and Honey figured she had to be feeling the pressure now she was about to ride.

"I'm just going to go get Tybalt's anti-sweat rug," Malory said after she'd slackened the gelding's girth. "I'll be back in a second."

Paris Mackenzie from Curie was due to ride after Lynsey. She trotted past on Whisper with a determined expression on her face. A short while later Lynsey led Bluegrass up and secured him to the wall.

"Did you go clear?" Dylan asked.

Lynsey looked pained. "Please. If you and Malory went clear, then do you even have to ask if I did?" She slackened Bluegrass's girth and then disappeared into the barn.

Riding the A circuit this summer hasn't done her ego any favours, Honey thought. She knew that Lynsey was having a dig at Tybalt's past unreliability and Morello's lack of breeding more than their riders' skill, but that didn't make it any less of a cheap shot.

Honey and Dylan walked over to the entrance with Lani, and as Paris rode past, the loudspeaker blared. *Paris Mackenzie, Curie, two faults on Whisper, one minute thirteen; now riding, Lani Hernandez, Adams, on Colorado.*

Dylan patted Colorado's neck. "Go get 'em."

"You could make it an all-Adams team." Honey smiled up at Lani. "Good luck!"

Malory came rushing up just as Colorado took the first fence. She groaned as Lani picked up an immediate four faults. Honey couldn't see what had made Colorado tip the top pole. Neither he nor Lani had done anything obviously wrong, but there had been enough clear rounds for this to write them out of the competition.

"Bummer," Dylan said. "I know she didn't make a big deal out of getting on to the team, but she's still going to be disappointed."

Honey didn't know if Lani would feel better or worse that over the rest of the course she and Colorado turned in a performance that was both fast and clear. As they rode out of the arena Lani pulled a face at her friends. "Always the bridesmaid and never the bride," she joked. "I'm going to untack him and then we'll be back to see you two riding your lap of honour."

"Don't jinx us," Dylan warned, but as the other competitors took the course, there were only two more clear rounds.

"That makes seven clear rounds altogether," Honey commented. There had been a glut of rounds with faults picked up at the wall.

Dylan's face had lost its colour at the prospect of a jump-off for a full place on the team. "So it's me, Mal, Lynsey, Tessa Harding from Meyer, Heidi Johnson from Potter, and Lucy Price and Joanna Boardman from the seventh grade."

"We'd better get the horses ready," Malory suggested.

Ms Carmichael stopped them as they walked out of the entrance. "Well done, girls!" She brushed off a strand of hay that was clinging to Dylan's black show coat. "Can't have you looking anything less than perfect for your first appearance as a full team member."

Dylan swapped a confused glance with Malory. "What about the jump-off? There were seven clears."

"Weren't you paying any attention to the times? There was a clear divide between the top four and bottom three rounds. Tessa, Heidi and Joanna had the same time so they're in a jump-off for the reserve position, but the rest of you have done enough to earn your place." Ms Carmichael smiled. "Now go get those ponies!"

Joanna Boardman ended up winning the reserve place by riding another clear round on her own pony, Calvin. "Congratulations," Honey called.

"Thanks," Joanna said, her face flushed with excitement.

Ms Carmichael joined them. "Well done, everyone. I'm about to go in so I can officially present you with your ribbons, but before I do, I want to let you know that Malory will be team captain this year."

Malory turned bright red, but before she could say anything, Lynsey objected. "I rode the fastest round and I have far more experience than Malory. You can't make her captain over me. I rode the A circuit this year and all she made it to was a local novice show in Cheney Falls!"

Honey gulped. Surely Lynsey had gone too far this time?

Ms Carmichael stood back and looked at the new junior jumping team. "As I'm sure you all know, the school's motto means Truth, Wisdom and Loyalty. Being a team member means you are an ambassador for Chestnut Hill. I have to have confidence that any person picked to be captain can show loyalty to the rest of their team, even when they may not turn in the best of performances." She smiled. "I just want you to know that I think we have one of the strongest junior jumping teams that Chestnut Hill has ever had. I can't wait to unleash you on our opposition!"

Lynsey's back was stiff and her face expressionless as she allowed Malory to ride first into the arena, in sharp contrast to Dylan's jubilant grin as she rode into the arena in third place.

"I don't know about you but I think Lynsey could do

with a Team Adams cheer," Lani murmured to Honey. "I almost feel sorry for her!"

Honey agreed. With Malory as captain and Dylan winning a full place on the team, they had more than enough to cheer about. But as she made her way up the stairs to the viewing gallery, she knew that she would have a hard time throwing herself one hundred per cent into the celebrations.

How could she when Minnie was about to leave Chestnut Hill for ever and, with one word to Patience, Honey could stop it from happening?

Chapter Eleven

Sunday felt as if it would never end. Honey went for a swim in the indoor pool before brunch and then decided to go for a long walk in the school grounds. Usually she would spend most of the day down on the yard but right now that was the last place she could face.

She walked along the woodland tracks where she had ridden so many times on Minnie. *If Minnie goes, how long will it be before I can come this way and not think about the way she loved to canter along the path?* Honey pulled her jacket closer against the crisp afternoon air and kicked up a pile of fallen leaves. They showered back down to the ground in a kaleidoscope of colour, and as she continued her walk, they rustled under her feet. Honey could almost hear Minnie's hooves crunching over the leaves as she imagined riding her along the tree-lined track.

In the end she gave up on her walk and turned back for the dorm house. There were too many memories here. She needed to lose herself in a book or a movie that didn't have any equine associations.

* * *

Dylan was on the phone to her father in the common room. "Yes, I can't wait. Thanks for making all of the arrangements for the sale, Dad." She snapped the phone closed.

"So when's Starlight coming?" Honey asked, shrugging off her jacket. She guessed that was what Dylan had been discussing.

Dylan looked awkward. "I'm not sure of the exact date."

She must feel bad talking about her pony arriving when she knows that any day soon Minnie will be going. But that was the last thing Honey wanted. She sat down on the sofa alongside Dylan. "You must be so excited about having your own pony."

"Uh huh." Dylan was noncommittal. Then she turned to face Honey. "I guess the truth is that I already feel like I do have my own pony. It's probably because Morello belongs to Aunt Ali, so he's already in the family. Don't get me wrong, I know that he's a Chestnut Hill pony and is there for everyone, but because I've got such a bond with him, I don't feel the need to have another pony exclusively as my own. Does that make sense?"

Honey nodded. It was exactly how she had felt about Minnie, although the fact that the pony belonged to Patience had presented more of an issue for her. If Minnie had been owned by a member of her family, or even by Chestnut Hill, she would have felt more secure. *If I tell Patience that I'll go along with her story, how secure would I ever be? And how could I ever live with myself knowing that the price for Minnie was paid by Mr Rivers, not me?* For a moment she felt like confiding in Dylan, but Dylan was still on a high from her success yesterday and the anticipated arrival of Starlight Express. There was no way Honey could bring herself to spoil her friend's happiness.

She got up and walked over the cabinet where the DVDs were stored. "Do you want to watch a movie with me?"

"Great idea," Dylan enthused. "I'll round up the others and grab some snacks from the student centre while you decide what to watch."

"OK." Honey turned her attention to the vast stack of movies. The first film she saw was *The Horse Whisperer.* She picked it up and resolutely pushed it to the back of the cabinet. Then she leaned her head against the side of the cupboard, the smooth wood cool against her brow. She was starting to realize that it was impossible to escape from horses at Chestnut Hill.

"Honey! Come look!"

Honey quickly pushed the back of her stud earring on and hurried over to the window. Lani pointed. They could just see the front of Old House from their room and there, parked up on the gravel drive, was a police car.

Two uniformed officers were walking up the front steps to the House. Honey and Lani stared at them as they disappeared from sight. "Do you think someone's gone to Dr Starling about Patience and Daniel?" Lani gasped.

Honey felt her stomach twist. "If the police are involved then Daniel might end up in loads of trouble." She turned to Lani in dismay. "I can't let that happen!"

Lani squeezed her shoulders. "Sorry, Hon, but it's not in your hands."

Honey stared at her friend. *Yes it is!* She had to speak to Patience. She had to tell her there was no way she would go along with her lie. No matter how much it would break her heart saying goodbye to Minnie, she had to put Daniel's reputation first.

Lani walked away from the window. "I guess someone should warn Patience the police are here. Somehow I can't help feeling she's brought all this on herself. This is all down to her spreading rumours around the school." She picked up her school bag. "Come on, or we'll be late for chemistry."

"You never believed her story, did you?" Honey asked.

Lani looked over her shoulder and met Honey's gaze. "Not for a moment."

Honey felt numb with misery. How would her friends react when they found out that she'd sat on the truth?

Dylan and Malory were waiting for them in the foyer so they could walk over to the science block together. When Lani told Dylan and Malory about the latest development they both looked worried.

"This is getting way intense," Dylan said. "I hope Patience is ready for the fallout."

157

This is all my fault. If only I'd spoken up straight away, things wouldn't have reached this level.

As they entered the science block, Honey felt her earring loosen. She reached up and realized that the back had fallen off. She couldn't have secured it properly earlier. "Guys, I'll catch you up. I just want to scout around for the back of my earring," she told them.

"Don't be long," Dylan warned. "You know how Marshy gets if any of us are late."

Honey dropped back and began to hunt the tiled foyer floor. As she was peering behind the umbrella stand, she noticed Patience walk through the double doors.

"I need to talk to you," she hissed.

"It will have to wait. I'm not getting a detention for turning up late to chemistry," Patience told her.

Honey reached out and grabbed Patience's arm. "Listen! The police are here. Dr Starling must have called them after she heard the rumours you've been spreading around the school."

Patience paled.

"Come on," Honey said, pulling her out of the science block. They headed down to the lake, where they were least likely to be caught by a member of staff.

"I've clearly got you all wrong," Patience said shakily as they sat on a bench that was hidden by large shrubs. "I never had you down as a rule breaker."

"It takes something pretty important," Honey admitted. "Which this is. Listen, Patience. This has got totally out of control. Whatever you think Daniel felt for you, the truth is that he never acted inappropriately at all. You've made up a lie which could end his career. You have to go to Dr Starling now and tell her the truth." She hesitated. "I'll come with you if you want." She felt more than a little responsible for the situation. If she had spoken up sooner, the rumours would have been quashed before reaching the principal.

"Oh, get over yourself," Patience snapped. "Why don't you say what you really mean? You'll come with me as long as I agree to drop Minnie's sale."

Honey stared at Patience. The thought hadn't even crossed her mind.

Patience narrowed her eyes. "I've got a different offer. You can tell Dr Starling that you overheard Daniel saying he had feelings for me."

Honey jumped up. "I'm going to pretend I didn't hear that."

Patience scrambled to her feet. "Listen, Honey." She placed her hand on Honey's arm and smiled. "You love Minnie, right? If you do this for me, I'll tell my dad I want to give Minnie to you."

Honey swallowed. "No," she replied hoarsely. "You're asking me to wreck Daniel's career. Even if I was tempted to do that, it would make me a person who wasn't worthy of owning Minnie."

"Oh, get a life," Patience said witheringly. "She's just a horse."

Honey had heard enough. "I'm going to see Dr Starling. It will probably look better on you if you come with me. But whatever you choose to do, I'm going to put everything straight."

"You'll get into trouble too. I'll make sure Dr Starling knows you knew the truth and didn't say anything," Patience said desperately.

Honey shrugged. "Do you think I haven't already worked that one out for myself?"

She headed back to campus and thought for one moment that Patience wasn't going to come with her. Then she heard the sound of running feet along the path behind her.

"Wait up," Patience called.

They walked to Old House in silence. As Honey knocked on the principal's outer office door, she felt her heart begin to race. She couldn't bear the thought that she was about to earn Dr Starling's disapproval.

"Come in," Mrs Danby, Dr Starling's assistant, called.

Honey glanced at Patience and was taken aback at how pale she looked. "It will be OK," she promised.

She opened the door. "We've come to see Dr Starling," Honey said.

Mrs Danby frowned. "Shouldn't you be in class? Dr Starling's busy right now. The police are with her discussing the school's security measures."

Honey felt the tension rush out of her. "Security?" she repeated in relief.

"Yes. You can wait if it's important, but if it's not I suggest you get to class and come back later."

"We'll come back," Patience said quickly. "Come on, Honey."

They hurried from the room. As soon as they stood in the corridor Patience closed her eyes and leaned back against the wall. "That was close."

"Too close," Honey agreed. "But if you don't stop everyone talking about Daniel, Dr Starling's bound to hear and then this will be for real."

Patience opened her eyes and shot Honey a look of pure dislike. "I was getting bored with the whole thing anyway. I had totally intended telling everyone it was one giant windup in the common room tonight. Why did you have to freak out at the sight of a police car? And now we're going to get a detention for missing chemistry. Way to go, Honey!"

Honey shook her head. Patience was beyond belief. "Just make sure you do tell everyone or, first thing tomorrow, I'm going to see Mrs Herson."

"Whatever." Patience ran her fingers through her hair. "Oh, by the way, I almost forgot to tell you. I got a call from my dad this morning. He sent out papers to Minnie's new owners today."

Honey felt her knees go weak. "Minnie's been sold?" she whispered.

"Yesterday," Patience said airily. "Catch you later." She shouldered her bag and headed down the corridor.

Honey stared after her. All the time Patience had been making promises in return for Honey's help in covering up her story, she had known that the mare had been sold.

Chapter Twelve

"Where did you get to?" Dylan asked as Honey joined them in the cafeteria.

Honey sat down alongside Malory and shook her head at her friend's offer to get her a snack. Right now she couldn't eat a thing.

"Wherever it was obviously wasn't great. You look awful," Lani said with her usual directness.

Honey rubbed her temples. "I've got something to tell you all. It's something I should have told you a few days ago when Patience started to spread rumours about Daniel. . ." Her voice broke off.

"We're listening," Malory encouraged. She reached out to cover Honey's hand with her own.

Honey took a deep breath, drawing strength from her friends' support.

"I knew all the time that Patience was lying. I overheard a conversation she had with Daniel. He told her that he was leaving the school because he'd just got engaged. Patience freaked out and ran off. She didn't know I'd heard anything and when I found her crying in her room, she pretended she was upset about Daniel turning her down when she asked him to dance." Honey sighed. "I felt sorry for her so I helped her patch up her make-up and when we went back to the hall we both acted like nothing had happened. I couldn't believe it the next day when she made up such an awful lie about Daniel."

Dylan slipped her arm around Honey's shoulders. "Why didn't you tell us? We'd have helped you challenge Patience."

Honey dropped her head and stared at Malory's hand resting on her own. "That's the worst bit. I did challenge her. Patience said that if I didn't say anything, she wouldn't sell Minnie."

"That sounds in keeping with Patience's delightful personality." Water could have frozen in the chill of Lani's voice.

"I can't believe it took me a couple of days to work out what I should do." Honey felt her cheeks burn. "I hoped the rumours would just die down and then no harm would have been done and Minnie would have stayed. But when I saw the police car this morning, I knew I had to tell the truth. I made Patience come with me to see Dr Starling."

"That was brave," Malory said.

Honey smiled weakly. "Would you believe that the police were only here to inspect security?"

"So you didn't see Dr Starling?" Dylan questioned.

Honey shook her head. "No, but I've given Patience till the end of the day to set the record straight. If she

163

doesn't, I'm going to Mrs Herson and telling her everything."

"Good for you." Malory squeezed her hand.

"And you shouldn't beat yourself up for agonizing over what you should do. We all know how much Minnie means to you," Lani said. "You thought the rumours would die down. The moment Daniel was really threatened you did the right thing."

And Minnie was sold anyway. Honey's throat closed and to her horror she felt her eyes fill with tears.

"What is it?" Malory's eyes widened in alarm. "What's wrong, Honey?"

"Minnie. . ." Honey forced herself to speak. "Minnie's been sold. All along, Patience had no intention of keeping her."

Malory slipped her arm around her. "Oh, Honey, I'm so sorry."

"When is she going?" Lani got up from her chair and came to hug her.

"I don't know." Honey sighed. "But I suppose it will be soon."

Dylan leaned forward and took her hand. "You have to have one last ride on Minnie. You can't let her go without saying a proper goodbye. I understand your reasons for not wanting to see her, but I really believe that if you let her go without one final ride you'll always regret it."

"Dylan's got a good point," Malory said softly.

Honey felt torn. But the thought of never seeing Minnie again hurt more than the thought of saying goodbye.

"I'll go over to see Aunt Ali now and arrange it for after study hall." Dylan pushed back her chair. "You're doing the right thing, I promise."

Honey slowly pulled on her jodhpurs and boots. It was the first time she'd ever changed into her riding clothes without feeling excited about the ride that lay ahead. She picked up her hat and as she headed to the door, the most recent picture she had taken of Minnie caught her eye. She gazed at the photo on the pinboard which showed the mare cantering in the paddock, her tail kinked, her mane flowing back. She looked every inch a dream pony. *And that's all she's about to become. A memory, a distant dream.*

Honey flicked off the light and closed the door. Lani, Malory and Dylan had already gone down to the yard. Dylan had gone all mysterious and talked about getting things set up. Honey didn't know what her friends had planned but she hoped it was low key. This was going to be hard enough without any extra fuss. She just wanted one last quiet moment with Minnie.

The early evening light was turning to dusk and as Honey headed down to the yard, she noticed that the outdoor arena was lit up. Lani and Malory were sitting on the fence and Dylan was standing in the middle of the arena holding Minnie.

Honey's heart ached when she saw the mare. Minnie raised her head and gave a pleased whicker when she recognized Honey. Dylan pulled down Minnie's stirrups as Honey approached. "Take all the time you need," she murmured.

If only I could, I'd take all the time in the world and never let her go, Honey thought as Minnie gently nuzzled her shoulder.

With her heart feeling as if it were about to burst, Honey mounted. Classical music filled the arena and Honey glanced across to see that Lani and Malory had a portable CD player balanced across their legs. Honey felt a wave of emotion. Only her friends could pitch this final ride so perfectly. She should never have doubted them.

Honey squeezed Minnie and the pony responded by walking towards the outside of the arena. Minnie arched her neck and her movement elevated without Honey giving her any signals. It was as if she was ready to dance to the music.

"Go on then, girl, this will be our last dance together," Honey whispered. Minnie broke into a trot and as they turned down the diagonal Honey could almost believe they were floating. Despite her misery, her heart lifted and for a brief moment she closed her eyes and lost herself in the moment. Minnie's stride was smooth and fluid, like sailing on a sea of silk.

By the time they reached the end of the arena, Honey could feel tears streaking down her cheeks. "Enough, Min, enough," she sobbed. Leaning forward, she threw her arms around Minnie's neck. "No other pony will ever mean to me what you do," she promised. "I'll never forget you, never."

Quitting her stirrups, she slid out of the saddle and leaned against Minnie's shoulder, wondering how she would ever find the strength to walk away.

"Honey?" Dylan's voice was gentle as she joined them. "Why don't you put her headcollar on and take her back to her stall?"

Honey stared at her friend. She couldn't work out why Dylan was suggesting she untacked Minnie right now.

Without another word Dylan handed her a leather headcollar.

It wasn't Minnie's usual tack. Had her new owner sent it over already? Honey looked at the nameplate, which had Minnie's name engraved on it.

Moonlight Minuet ~ Honey Harper.

"I don't understand," she whispered. She wiped her eyes and looked at the nameplate again.

Dylan grinned. "It wasn't supposed to make you cry!"

"What's going on?" Honey said in bewilderment as Lani and Malory rushed over from the fence to hug her.

"The person who bought Minnie was my dad," Dylan explained. "It was something you said that decided me. Do you remember? You said Morello and I would always have a special bond but when Starlight Express arrived, he'd be the one I'd ride most. And I don't want to ride another pony. Why would I, when I have such a great relationship with Morello? But since Dad had offered to buy me a pony, I thought I could kill two birds with one stone. I could have a new pony *and* keep riding Morello. That's because you'll be the one riding Minnie for me."

"There's more!" Malory laughed.

"Yeah, tell her Dyl," Lani encouraged.

"I was just getting around to it before you guys butted in," Dylan told them.

Honey felt as if her legs were going to buckle.

"I want you to have the security that Minnie's yours and she's not suddenly going to be taken away from you, so my dad's been in contact with your parents and drawn up an official loan agreement. We'll renew it each year, but basically it says that Minnie is yours and yours alone to ride and care for." Dylan's eyes sparkled. "It's not been easy keeping it a secret, but it helped that you haven't phoned home in the last few days."

Honey stared at her. How could Dylan be speaking so matter-of-factly when she'd just grabbed hold of her upended world and set it back the right way again?

"She's not going," she said in disbelief. "Minnie's staying?"

"You deserve it." Dylan smiled. "You spend your whole life going around giving to other people without any thought for yourself. It's about time you get a turn to dip your hand into the candy jar."

And what a candy jar. Honey threw her arms around Dylan. "Thank you," she gulped. "You're a friend in a million!" She looked at Lani and Malory, who were beaming at her. "You all are."

"Just don't expect us to go giving you a horse as well," Lani teased.

Honey turned back to Minnie and dropped a kiss on her nose. "I don't want any other horse," she said. "Minnie's just perfect."

"Well, as soon as you can tear yourself away, how

about we go celebrate with a cup of hot chocolate in the student centre?" Malory suggested.

"Good call," Lani agreed. "We can toast Honey and Minnie."

"Yes, and to Mal becoming captain of the team," Dylan added.

"And Dylan rising out of the reserves," Malory put in with a smile.

Honey's spirits soared as she slipped Minnie's new headcollar on over her bridle. She knew exactly what her toast would be. She gave Minnie one last hug. "It will be one just for you and me," she whispered. "It will be to our future together. It will be to living the dream."

Look out for the next story in
Chestnut Hill

Chestnut Hill
A Time to Remember

an extract

Chapter One

"Enter at A, halt and salute at X, then track right at C," Lani Hernandez muttered. "Or wait . . . was it *left* at C? Aargh! Why can't I remember the stupid test?"

Lani was leaning on the fence of one of Chestnut Hill Academy's outdoor riding rings, staring at the rectangular dressage arena that had been laid out inside. The dressage test was the first phase in the first ever Combined Event to be held at Chestnut Hill; the new cross-country course would have to be completed next, and finally a round of showjumps at the end of the day. Crisp black letters on white boards marked eight points around the arena – three on the long sides and one each on the shorter sides – where transitions and movements had to take place.

Everyone around Lani was busily getting ready for their turn in the ring but she wasn't moving until she had cracked this test. She narrowed her eyes to look at the judge's table at the far end, where a rather stern-looking woman was drinking coffee. A Chestnut Hill upperclassman sat beside her, acting as a scribe and scribbling notes on the seventh-grader from one of the visiting schools who was just leaving the ring.

Lani's friend Malory O'Neill looked up from adjusting her tall riding boots and blew a strand of curly dark hair out of her face. "You start off tracking *right*," she told Lani. "The walk-trot test for the Starter class goes to the left. You should stop watching them ride – you'll only get confused."

"She's right." Lani's best friend and room-mate Honey Harper was standing nearby watching a couple of riders warming up in the next ring. She bit her lip, an anxious expression flitting across her heart-shaped face.

"What's up?" Lani asked.

"I'm just wondering whether I should have tried entering Starter rather than attempting Open on my first time out."

"Don't sell yourself short, Honey," Lani told her firmly. "You used to do one-day eventing back in England, right? I'm sure you and Minnie will do great."

"Oh, it's only me I'm worried about," Honey smiled, brushing back her blond hair. "I'm certain Minnie will be wonderful."

Her expression softened as it always did when she mentioned Moonlight Minuet, better known as Minnie. Honey loved the pretty, affectionate grey mare just as much as Lani adored Colorado, the buckskin gelding that she rode whenever she could.

For a while, it had looked like Honey would lose Minnie forever, as Patience Duvall, the grey mare's owner, was determined to sell her. Lani knew that the idea of losing Minnie had been close to unbearable for Honey, as she had already said goodbye to her first pony, Rocky, when her family had moved from England to the United States a year before.

Then Dylan Walsh had stepped in. Lani still grinned whenever she thought about it. Their friend Dylan was known for being impulsive and generous – but she was also known for being a first-class schemer! All those qualities had come together in the plan she'd concocted to keep Honey and Minnie from being separated. Dylan's parents had offered to buy her a show horse, but Dylan had decided she wanted to keep working with Morello, the lively skewbald gelding she normally rode at Chestnut Hill. So instead, she had convinced her parents to invest their money in Minnie and offer her to Honey on a long-term lease.

"Did I miss my turn?" someone called breathlessly.

Lani looked over to see her classmate Tessa Harding racing past, her competitor's number trailing from the pocket of her jacket and her curly brown hair escaping from beneath her GPA helmet. She had a slightly panicky look on her face.

"Don't worry, you've got one more to go before you. Good luck, Tessa!" Lani called, though she wasn't sure the other girl even heard her. Tessa was riding in the first Open group, which meant Lani's ride time was coming up as well. That reminded her – what the heck she was supposed to do after that first twenty metre circle at B?

A seventh-grader named Joanna Boardman rode past on her own pony, a cute bay Welsh cross named Calvin.

Both pony and rider looked a bit tense, and Calvin even let out a whinny to a horse on the far side of the arena, though he settled into a steady, reaching trot as soon as he entered the warm-up ring. Meanwhile, a group of three girls dressed in the hunter-green jackets of Two Towers Academy hurried past, leading their mounts behind them.

Lani decided the yard would look totally chaotic if aliens landed right at that moment, with hoofbeats and nickering horses competing with announcements over the PA system, and dozens of anxious competitors running around in search of boot polish or start times or one last check through their dressage test. Lani shivered as she felt the little thrill run through her that she always got when she was getting ready to perform, be it at a horse show, an important softball game, or in a really tough maths exam. It wasn't nervousness, exactly, more like excitement shot through with tension.

Malory came over and stood beside her, staring around the yard. "I still can't believe that this event came together so fast."

"I know what you mean," Lani said. "For a while it seemed like we'd *never* get to try out the cross-country course!"

At the start of the semester she had been eager to sample the new permanent fences that had been built on the school grounds the previous spring. However, a bout of heavy August rain – the remnants of a hurricane passing up the coast – had left the ground too soft. With the excitement of adjusting to being eighth-graders and everything else that went along with the new school year, Lani and her friends had almost forgotten about the as-yet-unused cross-country course.

But finally things had dried out enough. Lani remembered how amazing it had been the day she and her friends had arrived for their riding lesson and the Director of Riding, Ali Carmichael, had announced that they'd be trying out a few cross-country jumps that day. As Lani had expected, she and Colorado had taken to cross-country like ducks to water. The buckskin pony had pricked his ears as they'd approached the first obstacle, an inviting elementary-height log, at a brisk trot. He'd sprung over the small log with at least a foot to spare! His eagerness had made Lani laugh out loud and want to go all over again. He'd attacked the next obstacle, a stone wall, with equal enthusiasm, and in fact showed no hesitation at anything, from the ditch to the bank to the water complex. A few times over the course of the lesson Ms. Carmichael had even asked Lani to lead a couple of the less confident ponies over a jump.

That lesson had been just over a week ago, and was swiftly followed by the announced of the mini-event with several local schools invited to make the competition even tougher.

"It's no wonder I can't remember my dressage test," Lani said. "We have only been practising it for a week and a half!"

"You know what Mr. Musgrave says," Malory reminded her, referring to their strict but knowledgeable dressage instructor. "We're not supposed to practise the test itself.

Otherwise the ponies learn the sequence of movements and start to anticipate."

"OK, fair enough," Lani countered. "But I'm pretty sure even Mr. Musgrave would agree we are supposed to learn the test ourselves!" She glanced at the dressage arena again and frowned. It seemed ridiculous that she was having so much trouble keeping the test straight in her head. After all, it was just a basic pattern at walk, trot, and canter, with a few circles and changes of direction. "How do you guys remember it, anyway? Did you have the test tattooed on your horses' necks or something?" She brightened. "Hey, that's not a bad idea – anyone have a marker pen?"

Honey laughed. "Actually, I use a tip from my instructor back in England."

Before she could reveal the secret, Dylan came rushing up, her red hair flying and her green eyes wide and panicky. A bridle was dangling over her shoulder, the reins dragging behind her and threatening to get tangled up with her spurs.

"Have you seen Morello?" she panted.

Malory stared at her in surprise. "What do you mean? Haven't *you* seen him?"

"Don't tell me you managed to misplace your pony!" Lani exclaimed, reaching down to grab Dylan's reins and loop them back over her shoulder. "That's pretty bad even for you, Walsh!"

"I know!" Dylan moaned. "I'm absolutely positive I left him tied up outside the barn while I went to clean off his bit, but he seems to have turned into Soda!" She grabbed the bridle off her shoulder and shook it at her friends, as if to ward off any further argument. "Now, call me crazy, but I think I can tell the difference between a 14.1 hand pinto and a 15.3 hand palomino. . ."

Kelly Goodwin, one of Chestnut Hill's stablehands, hurried past in time to hear her. "Don't panic, Dylan," she said calmly. "I took Morello back to his stall to keep him out of the way. He was trying to untie his lead rope, and I didn't want him wandering around getting into trouble."

"Oh, thank goodness!" Dylan cried. "See? I knew I wasn't going crazy!"

"That's debatable." Lani grinned. "Only a crazy person would leave Morello tied up on his own like that. Everyone knows he's an escape artist."

"OK, so you've located your pony," Honey said as Dylan stuck out her tongue at Lani. "But I think you may have lost something else." She shot a meaningful look at Dylan's arm. "Where's your medical card?"

Lani glanced at the armband on Dylan's arm, which was empty. She patted her jacket pocket to make sure her own armband and medical card were still there. Over the past week or so, they had learned a whole new set of rules and regulations related to eventing. For instance, they all had to wear hard protective vests during their cross-country rounds, and an armband containing their medical information during both jumping phases.

Dylan glanced down and groaned. "The stupid thing keeps slipping out!" she said. "It probably fell off in the wash stall again. I just hope it didn't get soaked this time – it's already kind of smudged. . ."

"Relax. I'll help you find it." Malory checked her watch. "You're not riding until group three anyway, right? Me, too. That gives us plenty of time to track down your card."

Dylan didn't answer. Her eyes had narrowed and she was staring at something over Lani's left shoulder. Lani turned and followed her gaze toward the bleachers outside the far end of the ring. There were several dozen people gathered there waiting to cheer on the riders, but Lani guessed right away which ones in particular had caught Dylan's attention.

Malory glanced over too. "Check it out," she said. "Looks like Lynsey and Patience are making some new friends."

Lynsey Harrison and Dylan were room-mates that year, to their mutual dismay. The only thing the two of them had in common other than their room number was an interest in fashion.

And they can't even agree about that, Lani thought as she watched the tall, slender blonde girl throw back her head and laugh at something the guy next to her had just said. Nearby, Patience was chatting with another guy. Both girls were wearing Seven jeans and Prada boots, which stood out among the sea of riding clothes and school colours all around them.

"Who are those boys Lynsey and Patience are talking to?" Honey wondered aloud.

"I don't know," Dylan replied, slapping the bridle she

was holding against her boot. "But I know one thing. Neither of them looks like Lynsey's alleged boyfriend Jason!"

"Duh," Lani joked. "Jason has no interest in horses. How can you expect Lynsey to go without male attention for an entire day?"

Dylan rolled her eyes. "Well, she could have distracted herself by entering the event instead of being so stupid and snobby about it, for starters."

Lani grinned. "True," she said. "But you heard what she said. Poor, precious Blue might chip a nail . . . er, hoof!"

Lynsey had brought her own pony to Chestnut Hill ever since the start of seventh-grade. Bluegrass was an impeccably-bred, well-trained, blue roan pony gelding with a list of A circuit championships a mile long. Personally, Lani thought Blue would probably have a blast galloping around the cross country course instead of being stuck in the ring all the time. But Lynsey clearly considered eventing a second-class sport and wanted to make sure everyone knew it. Then again, Lani was used to that sort of thing from Lynsey. From the moment the snooty girl had discovered that Lani had done almost as much Western riding as English, she'd taken every possible opportunity to disparage that too.

"At least Lynsey came out to cheer us on today," Honey said.

Lani smiled at her. That was typical Honey – she always tried to see the best in everyone.

"To cheer us on?" Dylan said. "Or to flirt with cute

upperclassmen from Saint Kits?" She let out a snort. "I mean, come on – those guys have to be juniors at least! In fact. . ." Her voice trailed off and she marched off toward Lynsey and Patience.

"What's she doing?" Malory sounded worried. "She doesn't have time to get in a fight with those two right now – not if she wants to find her medical card, watch you two ride, and still get Morello warmed up in time."

Even from across the ring, Lani had no trouble hearing Dylan as she loudly greeted Lynsey and Patience as if they were her long-lost best friends. Both girls shot her annoyed looks, but that didn't stop her.

"So what did you guys think of that history test we had yesterday?" Dylan practically shouted, attracting the attention not only of Lynsey and Patience and their cute neighbours but most of the other spectators as well. "Looks like we're going to have to work a lot harder now that we're all in *eighth-grade*, huh?"

Lani grinned, suddenly realizing what Dylan was up to. The two Saint Kit's boys who both looked rather alarmed; it was obvious Lynsey and Patience had let the boys think they were older than they really were, with their high-end clothes and confident manners. Within seconds, both of them were pushing away through the crowd, leaving a pair of very disgruntled-looking Seven-wearing eighth-graders behind.

Before Lynsey and Patience could react, Dylan scooted off in the direction of the barn.

"I'd better go help her find that card," Malory said. "But don't worry, we'll be back to see you guys ride."

As she hurried away, the PA system crackled to life. Ms. Carmichael's voice floated out over the grounds. "The last of the dressage tests for the Starter group has taken place. Riders in this group can now proceed to the cross-country course according to your times. Meanwhile, we'll shortly be getting started with the first Open group's dressage. Please take note of your ride times and be ready to go when your name is called."

Lani felt a flutter of panic. The countdown had begun and she still wasn't ready! "So Honey, about that memory tip you were talking about. . ." she said.

"Oh, right!" Honey picked up her riding crop, which had been leaning against a fence post. "You just draw the test in the dirt like this. . ." She sketched a rectangle in the dusty ground. "Pretend the end of this crop is your horse, so enter at A. . ." She drew a line straight up the centre, and then traced a circle around to the right to indicate the pattern for the test. "See? That way you don't have to worry so much about remembering the letters. You just learn the pattern and changes of pace from a bird's eye view."

"That's a great idea!" Lani exclaimed, borrowing Honey's stick and having a go. "It makes the whole thing sort of like geometry. I should definitely be better at this than I am at memorizing a random bunch of letters." She glanced up at the dressage ring and wrinkled her nose. "If they had to use letters, why couldn't they at least pick ones that made sense? I mean, I don't care how many little rhymes Ms Carmichael tries to teach us – I'll never be able to remember A-K-G-H!"

"It's off A-K-E-H, actually," Honey giggled. "But I know exactly what you mean." Suddenly she broke off and her face lit up with a smile. "Oh, look, my family made it! Over here!" She waved vigorously.

Crop still in hand, Lani turned to see Honey's twin brother Sam and their parents approaching. Sam got there first. Lani stared at him, a little surprised by just how well he looked. He'd spent the past year fighting off leukaemia, and only within the past month had he been officially declared in remission. He was still too thin, but his blond hair was growing back and his skin had lost the sickly pallor caused by too much time spent indoors. It now had the same healthy glow as Honey's.

He looks amazing! Lani thought. *The way Honey talks, I was expecting him to look really ill. She's always saying how he's still weak and that it will take a lot longer for him to recover.*

"Taking up a new art form, are you, Lani?" Sam enquired, peering down at her scratchings on the ground. "Hmm. I wouldn't say that it reminds me of da Vinci. Picasso, maybe. . ."

Lani grinned at him. Her sense of humour had clicked with Sam's from the first time they'd met. Even though they didn't see each other very often, they always seemed to pick up right where they'd left off.

"Hey, what can I say?" she retorted. "Some of us have hidden talents."

"Yes. And some of us have talents that ought to *stay* hidden," he joked, returning her grin.

Honey rolled her eyes and poked her brother on the

arm. "Be nice," she chided. "Lani's in a panic about her dressage test. She's due to ride in a few minutes."

Lani checked her watch and gulped, realizing Honey was right. "Yikes," she said. She shot an apologetic smile at Honey's parents, who had just caught up. "Hi, Mr. and Mrs. Harper. It's good to see you but I have to run!"

"Yes, we'd better go get the ponies." Honey smiled at her family and gestured towards the bleachers. "You guys can sit over there to watch."

"The best seats in the house," Mr Harper joked.

Sam nodded. "Good luck, sis," he said. "You too, Lani. Not that you'll need it – Honey's always saying what a brilliant rider you are."

"Um, thanks." Lani was surprised to find herself blushing. Turning away to hide her confusion, she grabbed Honey by the hand. "Come on," she said. "If Chestnut Hill is hosting this event, we'd better make sure we show up on time!"